Tears fell on her pillow....

Through them, she had a blurry view of her Love-rock. That was a laugh. A lot of good a Loverock would do her.

For some reason, she pulled the covers back and went to get it. Then she put it under her pillow and lay down again. It was a crazy thing to do. But she didn't care.

Hey, it works with the tooth fairy when you're a kid, Callie reasoned. *And let's face it. I'm just like Sarah. I still make hopeless wishes on stars. And planets. And pieces of planets.*

She shut her eyes, and the wish she had wished so many, many times came into her mind once more.

Please, let me be beautiful. Beautiful, beautiful.
Even more beautiful than Laurel.
And, please, let Jake love me.

Mirror Image books
by Cherie Bennett and Jeff Gottesfeld

Stranger in the Mirror
Rich Girl in the Mirror
Star in the Mirror

Stranger in the Mirror

MIRROR IMAGE

Cherie Bennett
and
Jeff Gottesfeld

AN ARCHWAY PAPERBACK
Published by POCKET BOOKS
New York London Toronto Sydney Singapore

AN ARCHWAY PAPERBACK *Original*

An Archway Paperback published by
POCKET BOOKS, a division of Simon & Schuster Inc.
1230 Avenue of the Americas, New York, NY 10020

Copyright © 1999 by Cherie Bennett and Jeff Gottesfeld

ISBN: 0-671-03630-0

First Archway Paperback printing December 1999

10   9   8   7   6   5   4   3

AN ARCHWAY PAPERBACK and colophon are registered trademarks of Simon & Schuster Inc.

Front cover illustration by Kamil Vojnar

Printed in the U.S.A.

IL 5+

for Serena,
whom we intend to keep
occupied with our books
for the next ten years

Chapter

1

"You're Laurel Bailey's sister?"

Callie Bailey pushed a stray strand of shoulder-length blond hair behind one of her ears and sighed. She had heard that question so many times in the fifteen years of her life that she knew exactly how many letters there were in the sentence.

Twenty-four. If you didn't count the apostrophes.

"Uh-huh," she said to the salesgirl at Threads, the popular teen clothing store. "How did you know it was me?"

"Because, like, your name is on your backpack," the petite girl said. She was a vision in Pepto pink, and her name tag read MEGAN.

"And that's how you made the mental leap," Callie surmised, nodding seriously. "Impressive."

"So, like, do you two have different fathers or

something?" Megan asked. "Because—no offense or anything—you definitely do not look like sisters."

"Have you ever noticed that when people say 'no offense,' they mean just the opposite?" Callie answered Megan's question with one of her own.

Megan frowned thoughtfully. "Um . . . no, not really."

"Look, Megan. Could you please just stick my clothes in a bag?" Callie glanced at her watch. The afternoon was getting away from her, and she still had to bike home and write her "Geeks Speak" column for the school newspaper. It was due at eight o'clock the next morning.

Megan picked up one of the black T-shirts Callie was purchasing and pointed to the black carpenter pants on the counter. "Black is *so* not happening now. That's why all this stuff was on the sales rack."

Callie leaned on the counter and peered through her black-rimmed glasses at Megan. "Since we've now spent what feels like an eternity together, Megan, I feel I can ask you a question. When you look at my current ensemble, what color do you see?" She straightened up and spun around.

"Black T, black pants, black hiking boots on a—no offense—kinda pudgy body," Megan replied, wrinkling her nose. Then her voice dropped conspiratorially. "Oh, I get it. You wear all black because it makes you look *thinner!*"

Excruciating.

"Contrary to what it says in your little teen mags, Megan," Callie told her, "some of us don't spend our lives obsessing about looking thinner. Some of us actually have better things to do. Also, I happen to like my clothes. They have a certain *je ne sais quoi.*"

"Jenny say *wha?*"

"It's French for . . . skip it. Look, you have a style of your own. Let's call it Automaton Person Pink. I have a style of my own. Let's call it Geek Chic. I like it."

"Whatever." Megan shrugged. "I was only trying to—hey, Ashlee, check it out, this is Laurel Bailey's sister!"

"No kidding?" Another salesgirl, tall, willowy, and with perfect long red hair, hurried over. Her name tag read ASHLEE. "For real you're Laurel Bailey's sister?"

A couple of customers turned around to check Callie out, too. It made her cringe slightly. It was bad enough that everyone at St. Charles Parish Regional High School knew that she was the younger sister of junior-class walking-female-perfection and successful model Laurel Bailey.

Did everyone in the New Orleans Center Mall have to know it too?

"So, if I could just have my clothes—" Callie began.

"Hey, I think we have some photos of your sister from when she did print work for us," Ashlee reported, rummaging under the cash register. "Yup! Got it!" She held up an envelope, triumphant.

"I've seen 'em, thanks," Callie said. "So if I could just have my—"

"Let me see." Megan pulled a handful of modeling shots out of the envelope and laid them on the

3

counter. "Unreal," she said breathily. "She's, like, totally my idol."

Callie looked down at the photos of her sister. Taller than Ashlee and slender, but still curvy. Long, straight golden hair. Huge blue eyes. High cheekbones.

None of which Callie would have in this lifetime.

Ashlee looked from the photos to Callie. "So, like, are you adopted?"

Callie was getting mad—but not at them. At herself.

Every time she had another you're-Laurel-Bailey's-sister? episode, she vowed she would not let the next one get to her. Her feelings would *not* be hurt. She really would not care instead of just pretending not to care.

And every time I end up caring, Callie thought. *But there is no way I'm ever gonna let them know how much it hurts me.*

"So listen, Megan, Ashlee—creative spelling on the name, by the by—I appreciate that you appreciate the perfection that is my sister. I'll be sure to pass on your heartfelt sentiments as soon as I get home. That is, if I get home in this millennium. *With the clothes I bought.*"

"No need to get huffy," Megan said. She stuck Callie's clothes in a Threads bag and handed it to her.

"Thank you," Callie said. "It's been real, and it's been fun. But it hasn't been . . . you know the rest." She headed for the doorway into the mall.

"Say hi to Laurel for us, okay?" Megan called.

Yuh. Callie just kept walking.

* * *

4

Callie turned down the volume on her Alanis Morrisette CD and studied her computer monitor. On it was her current column of "Geeks Speak." Her best friend for life, Addison Pate, loved the column but hated the title. Conjures up images of high tech, software, and all that, he said. But Callie loved the title, even though high tech was on her Stuff-I-Care-About list somewhere below, say, dusting.

What Callie cared about were books, music, movies, fighting for the underdog, her family—even, sigh, Laurel—Addison, of course . . . and Jake Moore.

The Jake Moore part was top secret.

Top-*top* secret.

Jake was a senior and as great looking a guy as Laurel was a girl. Plus, he was as cool as James Dean in those old movies Callie and Addison rented, like *Rebel Without a Cause*. Plus, he was the lead singer for Pisces, a very hot band.

Plus, he was Laurel's boyfriend.

Callie's crush on Jake was something she kept hidden from everyone except Addison, and he was sworn to eternal secrecy. She would *die* if anyone found out.

Of course, every time she saw Jake and Laurel in yet another lip lock, she died a little anyway. She was so tired of her sister getting everything, and her getting nothing, just because of some genetic fluke that gave Laurel perfect looks and Callie . . . well, Callie looks.

Sometimes Callie would lie in bed at night, staring at the ceiling and imagining that it was Callie-and-Jake rather than Laurel-and-Jake.

Ha-ha. Big joke, she thought. *I ought to give stand-up comedy a try.*

Back to real life. Hers, not her perfect sister's.

She turned her attention to her column.

GEEKS SPEAK #9

This geek booked it down to the video store this past weekend to rent *She's All That,* hoping against hope that seeing the movie on the little screen would take away some of the disappointment she had felt at seeing the movie on the big screen.

Not.

Query: Why is it that in the movies, a geek girl is always depicted as someone who, if you just change her hairstyle a little and take off her glasses, could be seen with the dancing babes in the next fine-guy-of-the-month video? And why is it that said geek chick, once said hairstyle is changed and glasses removed, then goes from miserable to massively jubilant? Mondo insulting.

Yo, world? Get a clue. Geek is chic. Say it with me and say it loud: I'M GEEK AND I'M PROUD.

The doorbell rang. Callie glanced at the clock. Nine P.M. Which meant Addison. He was ridiculously prompt, a kind of nice geeky trait, but sometimes a little annoying.

As Callie padded downstairs, careful not to step on the family cat, Jumby, she made a mental bet with herself as to what Addison would be wearing. They'd been best friends since the day in preschool when she used black paint to paint out her front teeth. After she had been sent to sit in the corner, he went and sat with her.

That day he'd been wearing outfit number one. He had three, he explained to her, the serious four-year-old he'd been. He rotated. Not because he didn't have other clothes, but because he liked those three best.

Now, in high school, his wardrobe had changed a little, but Addison still rotated three basic outfits—the blue one, the black one, and the brown one. The blue one, which everyone called #1, was blue jeans and a navy blue flannel shirt. The black one, #2, was black jeans and a black-and-white plaid flannel shirt. The brown one, #3, was brown khakis with a brown-checked flannel shirt.

He did change T-shirts daily, but since all his T-shirts were white, they didn't count.

I'm picking #3, Callie thought. *Khakis and brown-checked flannel.*

She opened the door. Bingo. #3. Khakis and brown-checked flannel. Above the shirt a thin neck, thin face, blue eyes, dirty blond hair slicked back, and black-rimmed glasses, adopted after Callie started wearing them. The glasses were an essential part of his own Geek Chic, and gave Addison a seriously retro fifties rock-star Buddy Holly kind of look.

Very cute, in a completely geeky way.

" 'Zup, Bailey?" Addison asked as he came inside.

"Won again. I bet three, you're wearing three."

"What'd ya win?"

"Intense personal satisfaction," Callie said as they went upstairs to her room.

"Thrilled to have contributed to your sense of well-being." Addison glanced at her article on the computer screen. "So, have you done your trig yet?"

"I was waiting to do it with you," Callie said, plopping down on her bed.

"Correction. You were waiting for me to do it." He sat in her desk chair. "You were probably too busy ditzing out about your sister's highly overrated boyfriend."

"Correction. I do not ditz."

"Alas, poor Bailey, when it comes to Jake, you ditz. What is it about girls and lost causes?"

"Jake is not a lost . . . oops."

Addison smiled smugly. "I rest my case."

Callie threw herself back on her bed. "I never should have confessed my deep, dark secret to you. You're not supposed to use it against me, you know."

"Sorry, I missed that bit of advice in the *Best Bud Handbook*."

Callie closed her eyes. "When I close my eyes like this, I can still see his face. Is that weird?"

"Yep."

Addison studied Callie as she lay there with her eyes closed. He wasn't about to confess that when he closed his eyes he could still see *her* face. She knew everything about him—except that. How could she be so smart and still be so dumb? And how could he be such a wuss that he couldn't point out what was right in front of her?

He was in love with her.

It was so obvious that it made him cringe.

How could she possibly remain so completely clueless?

"Addison, do you think there is any way in this universe I could get Jake to like me?"

Addison shrugged. "Got me."

She sat up and looked at him. "Exactly my point. I *know* I've got you. I *want* him."

Ouch. Major wound in the vicinity of his heart.

"Come on, Addison. You are by far the smartest person I know. Help me."

"All right, since you asked so nicely." He walked over to the bed and leaned over so that his face was an inch from hers. He would have given his collection of mint-condition Buddy Holly vinyl albums to kiss her.

But, of course, that was beyond impossible.

"The answer, Bailey, is *N-O.* No. *Nada. Nein.* You cannot get Jake Moore to like you."

She pushed him away. "Thanks a lot."

"You're welcome. Where's your trig book?"

"Used it for kindling. I figure, why not make those pages actually *do* something?"

"I'm not doing your homework for you, Callie."

"Why not? I hate it. Why should I have to engage in something I hate?"

"Because it'll be on your SATs."

"Good point," Callie admitted. She got up, closed down her column on the computer, and took a running leap back onto her bed. Addison spread his stuff out next to her.

"Okay," Addison said, "we have to answer the problems on page—"

There was a knock at the door.

"Come in and save me from higher math," Callie called.

The door opened.

Laurel. And Jake. Laughing. He was carrying her piggyback.

"Forget how to walk, Laurel?" Callie asked. She tried not to look at Jake, since she was sure her feelings for him were written all over her face.

"He wanted to prove he could carry me upstairs on his back," Laurel said. She slid off and gave Jake a kiss on the cheek.

"Why?" Addison asked.

Jake shrugged. "Just foolin' around. You know."

Laurel stood behind Jake and wrapped her arms around his waist. "So, we didn't hear anything from in here. We wanted to make sure that you two weren't doing what we were doing downstairs."

"With *Addison?*" Callie asked. "Get real."

"Also known as neuter-boy," Addison joked, to cover up his own embarrassment.

"Don't let her dis you like that, Addison," Laurel murmured. She wrapped her arms around Jake's neck. "I happen to think you're very cute."

"Then how come you're over there instead of over here?" Callie asked, an edge to her voice.

But Laurel wasn't listening. She was too busy kissing Jake's neck. He turned around and got very involved in kissing her back.

"Get a room," Addison suggested. He tried to stare at his trig book, but his eyes kept going back to Laurel and Jake. Same thing with Callie. It was like some terrible car crash; even though she knew it would make her sick to look, she couldn't stop watching them.

They were just so perfect together. So . . . so everything that Callie wasn't.

Please, Callie thought. *Just once, let me be the sister who gets the guy. Let me be beautiful. Let me have what Laurel has.*

Let me have Jake.

Chapter

2

Callie propped her chin up with her hand and stared at Mr. Livelli, her American history teacher, who droned on and on in a boring monotone.

Next to her, Alexis Monroe, the self-proclaimed coolest girl in the junior class—not to mention the shallowest and meanest—touched up her manicure behind her textbook. In front of Callie, Marley Wilson—his actual name was Matt, but he had changed it after a family vacation to Jamaica where he discovered reggae music and Bob Marley—furtively read a comic book.

In fact, as usual, only Callie, Addison, and Sarah Brown, daughter of the school's drama teacher, were actually paying attention. Mr. Livelli's class was the last of the day, and on top of that, it was a Friday. And on top of that, there was a major football game that night.

No way could nice, caring, *geeky* Mr. Livelli compete.

As Mr. Livelli spoke, he rolled two pieces of green chalk around in his hand, flaking chalk dust all over his dark pants. There were perspiration stains under the arms of his short-sleeved polyester shirt.

He screamed "geek."

Why is it that so many bona fide number-one certified-class-A geeks end up becoming high school teachers? Callie mused. *Is it in our gene pool or something? And does that mean that in ten years I'm destined to be a female Mr. Livelli?*

She shuddered at the thought.

"We're looking today at American heroes through our history. And not a soul among you would like to venture a guess as to why we choose the heroes that we do?" Mr. Livelli asked.

Dead silence met him.

"Well, let's look at some modern heros," Mr. Livelli prompted. "Maybe that will give us a clue. Jim, what's important in a hero to you?"

Jim Kagen, the handsome star senior halfback, who had been doodling in the margins of his notebook, shrugged his massive shoulders.

"That he have courage," he answered finally. "When it's all on the line. Like Michael Jordan."

"Courage is important to me, too," said Shari Burtrell. She was a vacuous cheerleader who sat in the back of the classroom. "Like, um, Jim. It takes a lot of courage to play a hard game like football."

Callie looked at Addison; both rolled their eyes. Neither could care less about football or the big game that night with whomever the big game was.

In fact, instead of going to the rah-rah game, they and Sarah—who was Callie's second-closest friend— were going camping on one of the bayous that led to the Gulf of Mexico. They planned to bring Addison's telescope. Callie loved to stargaze, and the forecast was for clear skies.

"All right, athletes," Mr. Livelli said. "So, Jim, who else might you say are heroes today? How about to young people?"

"Well, my little sister loves Ricky Martin," Jim said. "Also Britney Spears."

"My niece loves *Buffy,*" said Shari.

"Hoo-boy," Marley commented, in his fake Jamaican singsong. The fact that Marley was a white kid who lived in the suburbs of New Orleans didn't stop him from wearing his hair in dreadlocks and sounding like he was born and raised in the Caribbean.

"Matthew?" Mr. Livelli asked. "You have something to contribute?"

" 'Tis Marley, good sir, and 'tis simple, really. You Yanks choose your heroes on the basis of looks."

"Get a life, freak," Jim grunted. "You're as American as I am."

"Legally, yes," Marley admitted. "But what matters, 'tis what's in your heart. 'Nuff respect, man."

The class tittered.

"Well, on behalf of whichever country is fortunate enough to claim you as a citizen, would you care to expand on that, Matt—er, Marley?" Mr. Livelli asked. "You're being a little cryptic."

" 'Tis like this," Marley said. "Americans don't care about issues. You care about who turns you on."

"Go crank up the reggae," Jim snorted.

"Mr. Kagen, name-calling is unacceptable in this classroom," Mr. Livelli said.

Callie couldn't take it anymore. Slowly she raised her hand. The teacher nodded at her.

"Mr. Livelli?"

"Yes, Callie?"

"I think what Marley is alluding to, however obliquely, is what I call the Basic Babe Theory of American Heroes."

The teacher shook his head. "I don't understand, Callie."

"It's not very complicated," Callie said. "If you're a babe, you rule. If you're not a babe, you're toast."

"Don't you think that's a little harsh?" Mr. Livelli asked. "And perhaps a little bit of overgeneralizing?"

Callie turned to Shari. "Shari, tell me the name of one person who's been mentioned today in class who isn't a total babe."

Shari looked at Callie blankly.

"How about this, Shari?" Callie asked her. "How about a movie star under the age of twenty-five you would turn down on a date because he's *not* a babe?"

Shari thought for a moment. "I can't think of one. No, wait! How about Babe the pig? Babe is no babe!"

The class cracked up.

"But you see, that's my point," Callie said. "With people, babes get to be the heroes. Good-looking people beat the geeks every time."

"Gee, guess that means you won't be famous or a hero anytime soon," Alexis said.

"Aw, nice one!" Jim cheered. Alexis blew him an air kiss.

Callie whirled on her. "Listen, Alexis, you're—"

But the rest of her sentence was drowned out by the bell that ended the school day. The kids bolted for the door, and Alexis made sure to bump Callie hard, on-purpose-by-mistake, as she sailed triumphantly out of the room.

Sarah Brown's sweet, round face was illuminated by the dying embers of the campfire as she looked up at the stars.

"They're so incredible, aren't they?" she said softly.

"Yeah," Callie agreed. "It feels like you could just reach up and touch them."

"But of course you're not really seeing them. You're seeing the light that was shining light-years ago," Addison pointed out as he fiddled with his telescope.

It was late that Friday night, and they were at a private campground that occupied a point of land jutting out into the water near one of the bayous. There were four other campsites nearby, all run by a couple in their thirties who provided security and supervision. Callie had camped there, with her family or friends, since she was little.

"Saturn is high enough to see," Addison said, adjusting his viewfinder. Callie loved that telescope. She'd even contributed some of the money last Christmas when his parents bought it for him, so the gift was partly from her.

Sarah hugged her knees to her chin. "Do you ever wish on the stars?"

"Sure," Callie said. "I wish that Jim Kagen and Alexis Monroe end up living happily never after in a trailer park, with ten hyperactive kids of their very own."

"I mean really," Sarah said, her face still tilted skyward. "You know, a wish for yourself."

"Such as who you could get to fall madly in love with you," Addison said.

"So not funny," Callie called to him.

" 'Star light, star bright, first star I see tonight.' You know how it goes," Sarah said. She smiled wistfully. "I wish on stars all the time."

"Any of 'em come true yet?" Callie asked.

"No," Sarah admitted.

"Then I'd say it's not working too well," Addison said, searching for Saturn again.

"Just because a dream hasn't come true doesn't mean it never will," Sarah said.

Callie's eyes slid over to her friend, whom she'd known almost as long as Addison. Sarah was nice, sweet, smart, and a terrific friend. But she was also, Callie knew, the person you would least notice if you passed her in the mall. Her hair was limp, her face plain if sweet, and she had a kind of geeky overbite.

Sarah was also thin from the waist up and thick from the waist down. She was a wonderful actress, but she always got cast in a comic role or as an old woman. She never got to play the lead even though she was inevitably more talented than the person who got the part instead of her. And everyone knew it.

What hurt even more was that it was her own mom who was the drama coach.

"Theater is a visual art form," Sarah's mom was always saying to her. "I won't be doing you any favors if I pretend it isn't so."

Sarah was hurt, but she was a malleable girl. She went along with it. It was Callie who got incensed on her behalf.

"Someday you're going to get the leads you deserve, Sarah," Callie told her.

"Actually, that's not what I wish for," Sarah admitted meekly. "Now I feel too stupid to tell you what—"

"No, I shouldn't have assumed," Callie said. "What do you wish for, then?"

Sarah sighed and shut her eyes. "I wish to fall in love—with someone wonderful. Someone so handsome I couldn't breathe around him. And I wish for him to love me back."

Callie looked at Addison. She was waiting for him to make some crack about her and Jake. But he was still busy with his telescope.

Callie bumped Sarah's arm playfully. "It's a great wish. Honest. Sometimes I wish . . ."

"What?" Sarah asked. "I never think of you as the kind of person who wishes for things."

"But I do," Callie admitted. "I wish for—"

"You two ought to be wishing that you were looking through this telescope," Addison said. "Saturn rocks."

Callie and Sarah went to look through the telescope. It was set on a tripod, and Addison had tightened its connections so that the scope would stay fixed on the ringed sixth planet.

Sarah was the first to look. "Wow!" she exclaimed. "I feel like I could wish for everything in the world, looking at that!"

"Give Callie a look," Addison urged her. "In case it explodes in the next five seconds or so."

Callie got on her knees so that she could peer through the eyepiece more easily. She and Addison had spent hours together peering at the night sky, but the immense impact of celestial bodies never bored her. It was always dramatic.

"Awesome," she breathed. "The colors. The rings. It's so incredible."

"Nice, huh?" Addison whispered in her ear. He inhaled deeply. Callie always smelled like fresh flowers.

"Your breath tickles, Addison." She waved him away.

Saturn was just so . . . so perfect. And even though it was a planet and not a star, and even though she had gazed at zillions of stars with her naked eyes that night, she couldn't help but mouth silently the words to the nursery rhyme she'd learned when she was little.

> Star light, star bright
> First star I see tonight
> I wish I may, I wish I might
> Have the wish I wish tonight.

Please let me be beautiful, she wished. *Please let me be beautiful so that Jake could love me.*

Callie gasped.

"What?" Addison asked. "Are you okay?"

"I . . . I saw something," Callie babbled. "A red streak. It came out of Saturn and—oh, my God!"

She stared into the telescope and saw the red streak grow bigger and bigger. "It's heading right for us!"

"Very funny," Addison said. He gently nudged her aside so he could look through the telescope. "Like I'm really going to believe that—whoa! You're right!"

"What?" Sarah yelped. "What is it?"

Callie pointed toward Saturn. The thing—whatever it was—was now visisble to the naked eye.

It was coming right at them.

They stood there, eyes wide, mesmerized, as the streak came closer and closer still. Then they gasped as one, as the head of it burst into a zillion glowing pieces and chunks of flaming *something* fell from the sky.

It was as if the heavens were raining fire.

Chapter

3

🙰

Her eyes snapped open.

Suddenly Callie was wide awake. Alert. *Hyper*-alert.

She sat up quickly in her sleeping bag, heart pounding, filled with the eeriest sensation that something—some*one*—had compelled her to wake up.

But what? And why? It had to be very late at night or very early in the morning. She could dimly see the outlines of Addison and Sarah in their sleeping bags, both sound asleep, so they hadn't awakened her.

What was it, then? Had a raccoon sneaked into their campsite looking for food? Had she heard a night bird in the trees? Another weird object in the sky? The three of them had stayed awake until well past midnight, to see if the celestial fireworks show might repeat itself.

There had been nothing more, and there was nothing now. She was imagining things. That had to be it. She had just woken up early. Really early. Even though she adored sleeping late and was always the last one to get up and even then Addison had to bang on a pot and—

You're making something out of nothing, she told herself. *You're awake. Deal with it.*

Callie shimmied out of her bag—she'd slept in black sweats and socks—and pulled on her hiking boots. She stretched a few times, rubbing her arms to warm up.

I'll be Miss Wonderful and gather wood to make a fire, she decided. Addison would be shocked, since she never woke up first, and never, *ever* was the one to start the fire. Or make the coffee. So this time she'd do both.

The faintest traces of dawn streaked the sky as she walked the perimeter of their campsite, gathering kindling.

This is kinda fun, she thought. *I feel like Greta Girl Scout earning a merit badge in*—

Suddenly her whole body began to vibrate. The wood fell from her hands. She had the same eerie feeling she had had when she first woke up, an electric sense of being more alive, more aware, more—

Nuts. More nuts, Callie. You are losing it.

Shaking her head at her own theatrics, she picked up the wood and brought it back to the campsite. She busied herself with starting the fire, nurturing it until she was able to add bigger sticks and logs.

Then the same feeling came again. *Shimmery*, if she

was going to describe it. Which she wasn't. Because she would sound like a lunatic.

She'd go for a walk. A brisk, arm-pumping walk, like those jock nature-types did. That'd be good. Clear the mind and all that.

Good.

Addison and Sarah were still asleep. No point in waking them. She could only play jock nature-type for so long, anyway, so she'd probably be back before they woke up. She set off on the narrow trail that ran parallel to the shoreline.

The sun was coming up now, the air was crisp; she felt great. A couple of fish jumped in the water, and gulls circled overhead, cruising for an easy meal. Was it cool to be alive, or what? She picked up her pace—maybe she should take up speed-walking or something—breathing deeply. Yeah. This was kinda fun, actually.

She stopped. Inhaled again. What was that odor? Like grape juice and freshly baked bread. But who would be baking bread out here in the middle of nowhere? And there was some other smell, too. Burning plastic, maybe, definitely not something edible.

"Okay, this is bizarre," she said out loud. "I smell something weird." She stopped a second. "And I'm talking out loud to myself. Both bad signs."

A breeze came up, pushing past Callie out toward the water, moving the odor toward her from . . . where?

Inland. Somewhere.

Without giving herself time to think about it, Callie started bushwhacking through the brush, sniffing the air. She knew enough to watch for poisonous snakes—after all, she'd lived in bayou country all her life.

Bayou country, magic's right, some is black and some is white, her old neighbor, Mrs. LaFont, used to cackle. Mrs. LaFont had lived in a very old house down the street when Callie was little.

Someday I'll teach you the voodoo, Callie, she used to say. All the kids in the neighborhood thought Mrs. LaFont was nuts. Callie thought so, too, but she also thought she was fascinating, and she loved to hear her tell stories about what it had been like living on the bayou when she was a little girl.

One day, when Callie was ten, her mom had hugged her and told her that Mrs. LaFont had died. Her old house had been torn down soon after that. And the next year the Bailey family had moved to a new neighborhood.

Funny. Callie hadn't thought of Mrs. LaFont in years.

As she worked her way through the thick bush, the burnt plastic smell overpowered the good smells. Callie held her nose.

And then, as she pushed her way farther into the brush, she saw it.

In the center of a clearing, something was smoldering, smoke was rising in a semicircle around . . . something.

She edged closer, until she could peer into the center of the smoky ring. There was a crater in the center, not all that deep, maybe five or six inches—as if something had slammed into the earth and left this hole.

There was something down there.

Glassy. Tinted red, or maybe that was just the reflection of the reddish morning. A pointy end was sticking up toward her.

The object was smoking. Callie squatted down. Something compelled her to touch it. She held out her hand, moving it closer and closer and closer—

She pulled her hand back.

Hold on, Girl Genius, she told herself. *Whatever that thing is, it's still smoking. Meaning it's still hot. Meaning you get—duh—burned if you touch it.*

Except that as she had lowered her hand toward . . . *it*, she hadn't felt any heat at all.

"Yeah, we're having a voodoo bayou moment," she joked nervously. "We're also referring to ourself as 'we.' How very Queen Elizabeth. Shut up, Callie."

She took a deep breath. Then, very slowly, she moved her hand back toward the glassy object.

Smoke, but no heat.

No guts, no glory, Bailey. She reached down and carefully loosened whatever it was from the soft earth inside the crater. She got it free and held it up.

It glittered like a dazzling diamond, as the early-morning sunlight refracted through its prismatic surfaces into a million rainbows. It was tinted a faint red at the top. The size of a softball, it had a pointy bottom and four matching, glassy, oval-shaped sides that slanted outward and then dipped in toward the top of the object, where they all met.

When Callie figured out what it looked like, she laughed with delight.

The object formed a perfect three-dimensional valentine's heart. It looked very much like the sun-catcher that used to hang in her family's backyard. Only a lot more spectacular.

Callie held the object up, the shining surfaces marking a sharp contrast to the deep blue morning sky.

Unbelievable.

It was like some kind of dazzling cosmic valentine. Compliments of Saturn.

That has to be it, Callie thought. *This is from the meteorite shower last night.*

She couldn't wait to bring it back to the campsite to show Addison and Sarah.

That night, after Callie had come home from the camping trip and done all of her homework, she was in the family room chowing down on leftover pizza and reading the *Times-Picayune,* when a certain story practically jumped out at her.

She picked up the portable phone and quickly punched Addison's number in, then listened to it ring.

"Do your own trig, Callie," Addison answered.

"Very funny and I did it already, thank-you-very-much. Did you read the newspaper?"

"Why, are we at war again?"

"You're in a bizarre mood. Wait, let me three-way

with Sarah so I can read this to both of you." She punched in Sarah's number.

"Hello?"

"Sarah? Me. I've got Addison on the other line. Hold on, I'm three-waying you guys." She pushed the Flash button on her phone to three-way the conversation.

"A conference call?" Sarah joked. "How Hollywood."

"You guys have to hear this article from the newspaper," Callie said. " 'Meteor Over New Orleans,' " she read. " 'Late Friday night, police precincts in New Orleans received a number of frantic telephone calls reporting a strange object in the sky. A red-streaked meteor lit up the sky over southern Louisiana. Eyewitnesses report that the meteor exploded before it reached the ground. Scientists at Tulane University say meteors like this one, while not normally as spectacular as last night's, enter the earth's atmosphere every day—' "

"And the little green men seen walking around the French Quarter shortly thereafter claimed to be tourists from Texas waiting for Mardi Gras," Addison added.

Sarah laughed.

"So I guess my heart is a piece of a meteor," Callie said. "I'm calling it the Loverock. Isn't that cool?"

"Give it to your true love for Valentine's Day," Sarah said. "That would be so romantic."

Callie snorted. "Yuck."

"Oh, come on, it *is* romantic," Sarah insisted.

"Don't you think she should give it to her true love, Addison?"

"Not if he's at the movies with her sister," Addison mumbled darkly.

"What?" Sarah asked.

"Just a joke, not funny, never mind," Addison said quickly. Callie would kill him if he spilled her secret.

"Addison, if you are still in possession of the face that I almost just punched out," Callie began sweetly, "let me ask you a question. Should I call those guys at Tulane?"

"Nah," Addison replied. "Meteorites are a dime a dozen. Just put your Loverock on a shelf and admire it."

"Hey, remember when we rented that old movie *2001?*" Sarah asked them. "What if your Loverock talks?"

"I'll scream so loud that both of you will hear me with your windows shut—"

"And I'll run over to save you," Addison assured her. "In fact, I'll be awake all night, awaiting your scream."

"Whadda guy," Callie said. "Okay, don't forget the quiz in—yuck—physics, see you guys tomorrow."

Everyone hung up. Sarah went to take a shower. Callie went up to her room and picked up her Loverock, her mind on the guy who was, at that very moment, out with her perfect sister. She had no idea that at that very moment, in his home, Addison was lost in thought about Callie.

Trying to clear her mind from Jake, Callie went back downstairs to polish off the pizza, setting the Loverock on the kitchen table. Jake and Laurel stepped through the front door just as she took her first bite.

"Well, if it isn't the future king and queen of the prom," Callie quipped as they came into the kitchen to say hello. "How was the movie?"

"What movie?" Jake asked, taking Laurel into his arms for a passionate kiss. As much as it hurt, Callie couldn't tear her eyes away.

"You're *bad,*" Laurel told Jake when the kiss finally broke up. "You know I hate those teen slasher things, and you always want to see them."

He grinned at her. "Well, I didn't see much of this one, did I?" He kissed her again.

"What's that?" Jake asked, cocking his head toward the glittering Loverock on the table.

Callie shrugged. "Something I found in the woods."

Laurel held out her hand. "Can I hold it?" she asked, and Callie handed it to her. "It's beautiful! It looks just like a heart. Can you imagine having a tiny version of this as a necklace? Wouldn't that be pretty?"

"On you, yeah," Jake said.

Laurel handed the Loverock back to Callie, then Jake wrapped his arms around Laurel's slender waist. He gazed at her as if no one and nothing else existed in the world.

Callie felt as if a fist were squeezing her heart. *I deserve a guy like Jake. I do. No. Not a guy like him. There is no other guy like him. I deserve him. And I will never, ever, ever, ever get him. Ever.*

"Callie? You okay?" Laurel asked.

Mortified, Callie realized that tears had come to her

eyes. "Something in my eye, that's all," she murmured, brushing her fist against it. Suddenly the last thing she wanted was leftover pizza.

"I'm packing it in," Callie said. "Night, guys."

They might have said good night, Callie wasn't sure. When she reached the top of the stairs and looked back down, they were in heavy mack-mode again.

She went into her room, put her Loverock on a shelf and got ready for bed. When she had crawled under the quilt and pulled it up to her neck, she felt lonelier than she had ever felt in her life. Downstairs, Laurel and Jake were talking and laughing. In between there were long silences.

The silences hurt Callie most of all.

Tears fell on her pillow. Through them, she had a blurry view of her Loverock. That was a laugh. A lot of good a Loverock would do her.

For some reason, she pulled the covers back and went to get it. Then she put it under her pillow and lay down again. It was a crazy thing to do. But she didn't care.

Hey, it works with the tooth fairy when you're a kid, Callie reasoned. *And let's face it. I'm just like Sarah. I still make hopeless wishes on stars. And planets. And pieces of planets.*

She shut her eyes, and the wish she had wished so many, many times came into her mind once more.

Please, let me be beautiful. Beautiful, beautiful.

Even more beautiful than Laurel.

And, please, let Jake love me.

Chapter

4

$\mathcal{M}$onday morning.

As far as Callie was concerned, nothing in the world was worse. It meant the start of yet another school week, a week where people like Jim Kagen and Alexis Monroe treated people like her and Sarah and Addison like dirt.

The caste system was alive and well at St. Charles Parish Regional High School. There were the everythings, and there were the nothings. Callie was a nothing. There was royalty, and there were serfs. Callie was a serf.

And the queen of the school was her very own older sister, even though she was still just a junior.

Callie showered quickly and went to her closet to get some clothes. The closet was a sea of black. She liked black. It was also a sea of baggy, as opposed to being a sea of fitted or short. Showing off her body to the everythings and the nothings was not in Callie's game plan.

Plus, black reflected Callie's general disdain for, and contrast to, Automaton Person royalty, particularly Pepto-pink Automaton Person royalty. Few things, she thought, were more pathetic than a geek clad in a pink sweater set, desperate to emulate a crowd of students who would never accept her. Excruciating.

No one could ever accuse Callie Bailey of being a wannabe.

She grabbed a pair of black baggy jeans and was about to reach for a black T-shirt and black cotton vest to go over the T when her hand stopped, almost as if it were frozen in time and space.

Do you really want to wear that? she heard a voice inside her head ask. *You wear black every day. What are you, a little black-clothed rodent of civilization?*

"I like black. I wear black," she said firmly, reaching for the T-shirt again.

Bor-ing. Come on, Callie, live dangerously. Add color.

Callie stepped away from her closet and sat down on the edge of her bed. "I'm getting a very *Days of Our Lives* feeling, here," she muttered aloud. "I seem to have developed overnight multiple personality disorder."

"Callie!" her mother called from downstairs. "We're leaving in three minutes. There's traffic!"

Callie sighed. Her mother was dropping her at school that morning because Laurel had left early in order to go to an early meeting of The Saints Club. The

Saints ran everything at their school. You had to be invited to join The Saints. Laurel had been invited as a tenth grader.

And now she was, of course, The Saints' president.

"Callie?"

"Heard you, Mom!" Callie called back.

She got up and stood before her closet again. But she simply couldn't make herself reach for a black T-shirt. Instead, she went to her dresser and opened the bottom drawer, where she kept various articles of clothing and cosmetics that had been gifts from her well-meaning grandmother.

They were clothes that had never been worn.

Cosmetics that had never been used.

Callie didn't hesitate. She reached into the drawer.

"What is *that?*" Addison demanded as Callie sat down next to him in homeroom.

"What's what?"

"*That,*" Addison repeated, pointing at the T-shirt Callie wore under an unbuttoned black cotton cardigan.

"It's a T-shirt," Callie said, checking to make sure she'd remembered to stick her trig book in her backpack.

"Yes, it's a T-shirt all right," Addison agreed. "But it's pink. I repeat, pink. *Pepto pink.* Callie Bailey has never, to my knowledge, worn Pepto pink in her life. What happened, did you lose a bet with Laurel or something?"

"No, I didn't lose a bet with Laurel," Callie replied. "Don't make such a big deal out of it."

Addison nodded. "Fine. Cool, no prob here." He started clicking a ballpoint pen open and shut. "Pepto pink. I'm coming tomorrow dressed in Pepto pink. But I won't make a big deal out of it."

"Good," she said, timing her words with his clicks. "I won't. Besides, you're wearing something with color," she pointed out. "Outfit number one. Blue shirt. Shocking, boys and girls, don't you think?"

"Not shocking for me," Addison said. "But I'm not Callie Bailey, Geek Chic diva."

"My suggestion to you is, lighten up." She rummaged around in her backpack. "You want a mint? I've got some in here somewhere." She took out a couple of things and set them on her desk, the better to find her buried mints.

"Uh, Cal?"

"Uh, what? Ah, Tic Tacs!" She brandished the mints triumphantly. "Don't tell me that I'm disorganized. I know it and I'm proud of it."

Addison pointed to an item she'd pulled from her backpack. "Cal, what is *that*?"

"Looks to me like lip gloss. Cherry flavored." Callie screwed open the little pot, dipped her pinkie finger in it, and applied it to her lips, using the mirror on the bottom to check out her reflection.

Addison leaned forward and whispered to her. "Listen. You haven't by any chance seen my best friend Callie, have you? Because while the girl sitting in her seat may look kind of like her, she definitely is *not* her."

"Mmmm, yum, love the cherry flavor," Callie said,

dropping the gloss container into her backpack. "Now, what were you saying?"

"Oh, nothing." Addison smiled at her. "Notice how friendly I'm being. How accepting. It's the New Togetherness. You see, when you challenge the mentally confused or deranged, they can sometimes become violent."

"You are making a really big deal out of noth—"

"Callie?" Sarah Brown stood next to Callie's desk, her eyes huge.

"Last time I checked," Callie replied cheerfully.

"You're wearing *pink.*"

"Thank you for pointing that out, Sarah."

"Maybe we should check for a fever," Addison mumbled. He leaned over to put a hand on Callie's forehead.

Callie feinted away from him. "Addison, for goodness sake. Don't you know that that's the best way to get zits? Never, ever, ever touch your face with your hands!"

Sarah and Addison shared a look of horror.

"Look," Callie went on, "if you two want to make decent hygiene, a vial of cherry lip gloss, and a T-shirt that was a gift from my grandmother into a major deal, go right ahead. Or you could both just . . . get a life."

"Callie—" Addison began.

Ring! The homeroom bell sounded. Another Monday morning at St. Charles Parish Regional High.

Lunch.

Every lunch period at school—at least since she'd

started middle school four years before—Callie did exactly the same thing. She'd get into the hot food line, take whatever she felt like eating, and nab a giant cookie for dessert. Then she'd go sit with Addison and Sarah and maybe a couple of other kids at the Geek Chic table.

But today was different.

As soon as she hit the cafeteria, she looked around for her sister. There Laurel was, standing in the salad bar line with two of her gorgeous friends, Leesa Deerfield and Julia Birch. Leesa and Julia were seniors. The entire school—faculty and administration included—was in awe of them.

Callie went over to them. "Hi."

"Nice T-shirt, Callie," Julia said.

"Oh, thanks. Hey, Laurel, can I talk to you a sec?"

Laurel shrugged. As if by unspoken mutual agreement, she and Callie never talked to each other in school. It was one reason so many people didn't realize they were sisters.

"It's kind of private," Callie added.

Laurel sighed impatiently. "Be right back," she told her friends and got out of line. "What is it?"

"What are you doing after school?" Callie asked.

"You took me out of line to ask me what I'm doing after school?" Laurel echoed.

"Kind of."

"Let's see, there's a meeting of The Saints about the dance, and then I'm going home, and then I'm going for a run, and then I'm going to study with Jake."

Callie nodded. "Well, I wanted to know if I could go running with you."

Laurel laughed. "That's a joke, I take it."

"No, I'm serious."

"Callie, you hate to exercise. If our house was on fire, I think you'd *stroll* out."

"Look, if it's going to be too much trouble to run with your younger sister, I can just do it on my own."

Laurel put her hands on her hips. "This is definitely some kind of a setup. You're gonna pull a hidden camera out from behind a door and broadcast the tape on one of your geeky friends' cable-access television shows, and—"

"People change, Laurel," Callie said. "I happen to be completely serious. But if you don't want me to run with you, then—"

"Fine, you can run with me. I'm assuming this is a one-day deal, right?"

"No. I plan to do it regularly," Callie said.

Laurel looked aghast. "Are you feeling okay?" She went to put her hand on Callie's forehead.

"Please! Don't you know you're never supposed to touch your face with your hand? It's a zit-factory!"

The phone simply would not stop ringing.

It was after school, and Callie had changed into black gym shorts to go with her pink T-shirt. She'd been waiting for Laurel so they could go running. But every one of Callie's geek friends seemed to feel the need to call her.

What was up with the pink T-shirt?

Was that Chapstick or actual *lip gloss* she'd been wearing at school?

Was the rumor true that Callie was going running with Laurel? On purpose?

Really, people get stuck into such silly little molds, Callie thought as she buffed her nails to a clear shine and waited for the phone to ring again. *It's not like I turned into a different person.*

She frowned at her nails. Maybe they'd look better with a coat of sheer pink polish.

Laurel came home, quickly changed, then she and Callie set off on their run. Laurel kept waiting for Callie to quit. Only she didn't. In fact, she managed a mile before she stopped, keeling over and sucking for breath.

The next day she did a mile and a half.

The day after that, a mile and three quarters.

Thursday, two miles.

On Friday she woke up forty-five minutes ahead of anyone else in her household so that she could go for a run *before* school started, hoping that maybe after school she could do some training with the dumbbells and free weights Laurel had down in the basement.

That day when she got dressed for school, she wore a black T-shirt . . . with pink jeans, compliments of Grandma. The jeans were loose on her. And she wore makeup. And she had blow-dried her hair as straight as her sister's.

But to her friends the scariest change of all was that she had traded in her trademark black-framed glasses for some new silver-wire rims.

Everyone talked about her, but she didn't care. As for Addison and Sarah, the two of them were pretty sure that she'd lost her mind.

After school she decided she had to make a stop at Threads at the mall. The clothes from her grandmother would only last so long. She needed a few things. Cute things.

She walked into Threads and saw Megan, the salesgirl who had been so obnoxious to her.

"Hi," Callie said. "Remember me?"

Megan frowned a second, then her eyes lit up. "*You're* Laurel Bailey's sister?"

Callie smiled. "It's me."

Megan's jaw dropped open. "Wow, you look fantastic! Did you lose weight or something? Hey, Ashlee, come see Laurel Bailey's sister. What's your name again?"

"Callie."

"Right, right. This is awesome," Megan marveled. "I mean, gosh, Callie, I hate to say it, but you look *good.*"

Ashlee joined them. "Unreal. You do look good! What was your name again?"

"Callie."

"Right, Callie." Ashlee nodded. "Well, listen, I don't know how you did it, but you have totally lost that icky loser look."

Resentment flared in Callie for just a second. "As opposed to a totally icky loser personality, you mean," she said sweetly.

"Whatever," Ashlee said, shrugging. "So, are you shopping?"

Callie nodded. "I need some new clothes." She looked Ashlee over. Whatever else she thought of her, Ashlee looked fantastic. "Kind of like yours, maybe."

"How are you planning to pay?" Megan asked sharply.

"My mom's credit card," Callie said. "I told her I was coming here."

Ashlee put an arm around Callie. "Listen, Laurel Bailey's little sister, my suggestion is that you put yourself and your mom's credit card in my hands. By the time you walk out of here, you will rule."

Chapter

5

She heard the phone ring but decided to ignore it. First of all, it was probably for Laurel. Second of all, Callie was too busy looking in the mirror, admiring her abs.

Abs. She had abs. As in, discernible stomach muscles. Plus, her waist was a good two inches smaller, her bust fuller. Plus she'd lost twelve pounds. Twelve pounds. In less than two weeks! Okay, so she was working out with her sister every day, but it hadn't even been a month yet. But her body looked completely different. More like Laurel's.

In fact, a *lot* like Laurel's.

And then, there was her hair. Formerly okay-to-nice, now spectacular. She didn't even need the blow dryer to make it straight, shiny, and perfect. It just was. As for her skin, it was perfect and radiant, her eyelashes thicker and curlier. A makeup artist at the mall had done her makeup the other day, and Callie purchased every product the woman had used.

Frankly, though, Callie didn't need all that much makeup to look really good.

Addison, however, did not share that opinion. Neither did Sarah or any of her geek friends. In fact, when she'd gotten home from school that day, she'd run inside when she heard the phone ringing. When she'd picked it up and said hello, a voice hissed a single word, *traitor*, and then hung up.

Whatever, Callie thought. *People are so hung up on labels. They all need to know what box they fit into so they won't have to spend all their time biting their nails for fear of having no box at all.*

She put one foot up on her bed to stretch, and her gaze fell on the Loverock on her nightstand. Callie switched legs and stretched again. Funny how she'd actually slept with the Loverock under her pillow that first night and made a wish on it like some silly little kid.

The Loverock was beautiful. It had fallen from the sky. But it didn't *do* anything.

Actually if you're beautiful enough, you don't have to do much at all, Callie mused. *Everyone just automatically thinks you're wonderful.*

Laurel stood in Callie's open doorway. "Phone!"

"Who is it?"

"Pick it up and see, Workout Queen," Laurel said.

"We're going running right after this, right?" Callie asked as she reached for the phone.

"Yeah," Laurel agreed. "But if you start doing more roadwork than me, all bets are off."

"Hello?" Callie said into the mouthpiece.

"Callie?"

Callie froze.

She would know that voice anywhere. It was the voice she heard in her dreams.

But this made no sense. Never, ever in a million years would *he* be calling *her*. Not with Laurel smiling in her doorway.

"This is Callie," she finally managed.

"Jake. How's it going?"

"Okay." Callie walked to her chair and sat heavily on it. She felt as if she could hardly breathe.

And then it dawned on her. Baby-sitting! For Jake's little sister. It was Saturday. Jake and Laurel were going to some hipper-than-thou party that night. Probably Jake's parents were going out, too. Jake was about to hit her up to baby-sit.

Now it all made sense.

"Listen, Jake, the answer is yes. I don't mind baby-sitting for your little sister because I've been in serious spending mode lately."

Jake laughed. "My little sister has a sleepover tonight, I think. I wasn't calling to ask you to baby-sit."

"You weren't?" Her eyes slid over to Laurel, who was leaning against her door frame.

"Naw. There's a party tonight at Leesa Deer-field's house. We thought maybe you'd want to come with us."

43

"That is so not funny," Callie snapped.

"Well, good, because it's not a joke," he replied.

"Wait. You're saying that you and Laurel are going to a party at Leesa's, where you have to be a) a senior, or b) a card-carrying member of c) The Saints, or d) at least the cool crowd to get in the door. And you're voluntarily inviting me to come with you?"

Jake laughed. "You ready to party?"

"There has to be a catch," Callie insisted.

"Nope. It was your sister's idea. She told me that if she asked you, you'd say no on principle. But if I asked you, you might actually say yes. So, I'm asking."

It still didn't make any sense.

"Um . . . the phrase *dazed and confused* springs to mind," Callie said. "You really want me to come with you?"

She looked over at Laurel. Laurel shrugged.

"We really do," Jake said.

Callie cleared her throat. "Well, as luck would have it, my jammed social schedule happens to have a tiny opening this evening."

"Cool," Jake said. "You know where Leesa lives?"

"All of two blocks from here," Callie said.

"Right. Laurel and I are going to dinner first, so we'll meet you there at like, nine, okay?"

Callie bit her lip. *Reality-check time*, she thought.

Okay, so her sister was being incredibly nice for some bizarre reason and inviting her to a party with the beautiful people. Laurel was still Jake's date. Callie was still nothing more than Laurel's little sister. And the idea of facing the Jake-and-Laurel

show, plus all the coolest seniors, was kind of intimidating.

"Jake? Listen, I was wondering : . . ?"

"Yeah?"

"Can I invite a friend to come with me?"

"Sure. Leesa's parties are always a zoo, she won't
care. So, I'm glad you're coming. See you there."

"See you." Callie hung up. She looked at Laurel.
"Why are you doing this?"

"Because I'm incredibly nice," Laurel said.

"No, you're not."

"Let's say I've had a change of heart, then." Laurel
sat next to Callie on her bed. "You're changing, Callie.
For the better, obviously. I'm proud of you."

"Meaning that you weren't proud of me before?"

Laurel sighed. "Do you have any idea how many
times I've had people say to me, 'Callie Bailey is *your*
sister?' like I was supposed to explain why you were
such a geek?"

"Gee, that musta been tough," Callie said, seething.

"Yes," Laurel agreed. "But those days are over,
that's obvious." She stood up. "All The Saints will be
at the party tonight, all the people who count at our
school. Congrats, Callie. You're becoming one of
us."

The Baileys' house was nice, but two blocks away,
on the other side of Chenier Street, the neighborhood
changed from nice to spectacular.

That was where Leesa lived.

The party was in her Superdome-size backyard.

Rock music blared from an excellent sound system. People were dancing, eating, talking, making out, all in full party mode. Every senior who counted was there.

Callie had spent all afternoon getting ready, changing outfits over and over. Finally she decided to risk wearing one of the outfits Ashlee at Threads had practically forced her to buy but which she hadn't yet had the nerve to wear—a lavender slip dress with a sheer overlay with tiny lavender and pink flowers on the hem.

— At the last minute Callie grabbed a sweater to wear so she wouldn't feel quite so self-conscious.

It had taken a good ten minutes to get up the nerve to walk into Leesa's backyard. Callie was half-afraid Leesa would take one look at her and get that withering expression on her face that she usually got when she looked at Callie: the one that made it seem as if she had just smelled something incredibly noxious.

But Leesa had welcomed her with open arms. All the other girls, even members of The Saints, had, too. They'd said how cute she looked and how much she had changed and now they could finally see that she really was Laurel's sister, and why had she been hiding it all these years?

And guys flirted with her.

With *her*, Callie Bailey! It was as if she'd just been given a passport to a wonderful new world.

"Dance?"

He was tall and rangy, with a handsome face and short brown hair. Clearly, cool.

"Okay," Callie said shyly.

It was a slow song. As they danced, he told her his name was Brad, he went to high school on the other side of New Orleans, and he figured to be going to the University of Texas next year on a baseball scholarship. He didn't ask Callie one thing about herself, but Callie didn't mind. This was the kind of guy who wouldn't have given her the time of day before. Now he wanted to dance with her, wanted her to know all about him.

Amazing.

Of course, he wasn't Jake. She looked over at her sister. She was dancing in Jake's arms. But Callie was shocked to see that Jake was looking at her, Callie. Why? Very slowly Jake grinned at her. Callie turned away.

"So I figure I'll get drafted by the pros after my sophomore year of college, spend a couple of years in the farm system, and get to the majors that way," Brad was saying. "Playing catcher is murder on the knees, though. So if my knees go, then—"

Out of the corner of her eye, Callie saw Addison at the screen doors to the patio.

He was wearing outfit #3.

He looked scared to death.

"Excuse me," Callie told Brad. "A friend of mine just got here."

"Catch you later, then," Brad said as Callie hurried toward Addison. He called out after her, "Say, can I get your digits?" But Callie didn't hear him.

"Hey, big guy," Callie greeted Addison with a hug. He didn't hug back.

"This is a party," Callie pointed out. "As in, loosen up."

But how could he? Callie, the Callie he secretly thought of as *his* Callie, was wearing a sliplike thing that showed off every curve. And lots of makeup. And some intense perfume that smelled like hothouse flowers.

"Might I point out that you are unrecognizable as your actual self?" Addison said.

Callie folded her arms. "Oh, thank you *so* much. I live for your compliments. Come on, let's dance."

They joined the dancing throng, Addison doing his usual geek-type dance moves. Callie had always thought they were cute.

Suddenly they just looked dumb.

"Why don't you dance like everyone else?" Callie asked.

"Because I'm not everyone else," Addison said. "Neither are you. Though you seem to have misplaced that particular fact of late."

Callie sighed and kept dancing. She wasn't going to make a big deal out of it. "Isn't this fun?"

"More like some bizarre parallel universe," Addison said, taking in everything.

Suddenly, out of nowhere, Leesa appeared. She lightly put a hand on Callie's arm.

"Callie?" she asked, her voice all sweetness and light. "May I talk to you a minute?"

"Sure," Callie told her. "This is my friend Addi—"

"Privately," Leesa emphasized, interrupting Callie. "Let's go inside. Excuse us, uh, Addy."

Callie turned back to Addison and shrugged as Leesa led her away. They went inside the house, into the well-appointed family room.

"So, Callie," Leesa began brightly, "it's really great that you're here."

"Thanks for inviting me," Callie said.

"Aren't you sweet." Leesa smoothed an imaginary crease out of her pink cashmere halter top. "I just want you to know how proud we all are of the effort you're making in personal improvement. We've got our eyes on you, and . . . well, this is top secret. Between you and me, we're even talking about inviting you into The Saints."

"You're kidding."

Leesa smiled. "You're Laurel's sister. You're a legacy. With our help, next year you could be princess of St. Charles Parish Regional High. And the year after that, queen."

"That's—that's amazing," Callie said.

"Oh, sweetie, you deserve it," Leesa insisted. "Look how far you've come so quickly. There's just one little bitty thing. The geek has to go."

Callie wasn't sure she'd heard right. "Excuse me?"

"The geek. Your little friend. Addy, I think you said his name was. Honey, what were you thinking inviting a boy like that to a Saints party?"

Callie felt the blood rushing to her head. "His name is Addison. He's my best friend."

"Before, maybe," Leesa said. "But if you want to rule, you have to accept the responsibilities that come with it. We're all known by the company we keep, honey. So, do you want to ask him to leave, or shall I?"

Callie stared at her. "Do you have any idea how stupid you sound? You think he's going to contaminate your backyard or something?"

Leesa fluffed her hair. "Honey, I don't care what you think, I don't care how I sound, and I don't care what you think of me. This is my party. I say he's history."

"You know what? You're right," Callie said.

Leesa smiled smugly. "I knew you'd see it my way."

"And I'm history, too," Callie added. She headed for the patio doors.

"Whatever," Leesa called to her. "But just remember, you're never going to make The Saints by hanging out with a geek like him."

"Good," Callie shouted back to her. "Because I'd rather spend the rest of my life with him than hang around an insipid twit like you!"

She turned around, and there was Addison.

"I heard that," he said quietly.

"You know, suddenly I smell something really *foul*," Callie said to Addison as Leesa slipped by them. "What say we blow this shallow little stink-fest?"

"Lay on, Macduff," Addison said with an awkward sweeping bow.

They were outta there.

A half hour later Addison and Callie sat together on a bench that looked out over the water of one of the many bayous of St. Charles. As the moonlight glinted off the water, crickets chirped, katydids sang, and in the distance they could hear the mournful call of a whippoorwill.

"Thanks, Callie," Addison said, staring out at the water. "I know I said it before, but—"

"I told you, forget it."

Addison pushed his glasses up his nose. "I really don't know what we were doing there in the first place."

"What does that mean?"

"Callie, you hate those people, remember?"

She turned to him. "It's just as stupid for us to hate all of them as is it for them to hate all of us, don't you think?"

"Let's review, shall we?" Addison quipped. "You and I are weird, and we are proud of it. We are geeks. We do not fit in with the beautiful people. We like it that way."

Callie looked out at the water again. "Look, Leesa is a shallow witch. Shallow people suck. Ergo, Leesa sucks. But that doesn't mean they all do. I just want to be me, Addison. I just . . . I don't want to have to wear a label to figure out who I am."

Addison studied her profile in the moonlight. They'd been best friends forever. And even though she'd been acting kind of strange lately, her friendship meant more to him than anything in the world.

He hadn't planned on friendship changing to love. Romantic love.

But it had, and he had no idea in the universe what to do about it.

Ask her out? Just blurt out the truth?

And what, risk everything? This wasn't some teen TV show. Their lives didn't have scriptwriters and directors and executive producers. What happened if he asked her out and she *laughed?*

"I'm gonna head back," Callie said. "You ready?"

Was he ready? If he walked her home, maybe he'd come up with the right words to ask her out. He already knew what he wanted to do: the Dave Matthews Band was playing a gig in New Orleans, and he thought they could go together.

But not as friends. As a *date.*

The idea of actually asking her filled him with terror.

"Nah," he told her. "I'm gonna hang here for a while, commune with the stars, whatever."

"Okay. If you see any more exploding meteors, let me know." Callie gave him a friendly hug.

"You got it." He hugged her back. "I'll call you tomorrow."

Callie walked home, deep in thought about Laurel, and Leesa, and most of all, Jake.

Addison stared out on the bayou, trying to figure out how to let Callie Bailey know that he was in love with her.

Neither of them saw the jet-black sedan that stealthily followed Callie, lights turned off, all the way to her home.

"That's the girl," the driver of the car said as she drove. "She's the one I'm calling Subject One."

"Doesn't look at all strange to me," said the crewcut male in the passenger seat. "Just a typical teen."

"Blast that thing for falling out of the sky," the woman muttered, under her breath. "Incredibly bad timing."

"What?" said the man with the crew cut.

"Nothing. It's not important. Anyway, you can't always tell by looking, you know that," the driver reminded him. "Not in the early stages, anyway. You've ordered the yearbook photos of her from last year?"

"Yep."

"When we see them, we'll have some idea if she's really going to be Subject One," the driver replied.

When Callie got to her front door and let herself inside, the sedan sped off into the night.

Chapter 6

*L*ate the next morning Callie was nibbling a bagel and reading the newspaper when the phone rang again. Laurel was over at Leesa's house supposedly helping to clean up after the party (she hadn't been very happy with Callie about what had happened the night before), and Callie's parents were having brunch with some friends in New Orleans.

"Hello?" Callie answered, still engrossed in the movie review she'd been reading. It was the latest sequel to the *Scream* horror series.

If it's another of my geek friends calling to give me a hard time, I'm just going to—

"Callie, hi, I'm glad you're home."

She froze. She had to be hearing things.

It was Jake. Why would Jake be glad she was home?

"Um, Laurel's not here," Callie said.

"I know, she's hanging with Leesa and Julia."

Silence.

"So . . . do you want to leave a message for her or something?" Callie finally asked. "Gimme a sec, I have to get a pen—"

"No," Jake said. "Actually, Callie, I called to talk to you."

"To me," Callie echoed.

"Yeah. You looked great last night. Absolutely fantastic, really."

Jake is complimenting me? Jake?

"Thanks," Callie said softly.

"Really hot," he added.

This can't be happening. I must be dreaming.

"Thanks again," Callie said.

"So listen, Callie, I want to apologize. For what happened last night."

"It wasn't your fault," Callie said.

"That's not exactly true. I invited you to the party. And I said it was okay for you to invite whoever you wanted."

"I guess Leesa disagreed."

"Well, you know, Leesa's one of those girls who thinks she's all that 'cuz she's cute and rich. Lost of girls are cute and rich, it's no biggie, but she hasn't learned that yet," Jake said. "Anyway, I'm sorry you had to go through one of Leesa's postal moments because you brought a guy she didn't like."

"That's okay," Callie said.

That's okay? Callie winced. *Why does my brain turn to mush around him? It's so icky!*

"So, that guy—what's his name again?" Jake asked. "The guy you asked?"

"Addison."

"Addison, right. I've seen him over at your house a lot, but I always forget his name. So, are you two an item or what?"

"Please," Callie scoffed. "He's my bud. He's not exactly my type."

"No? So what's your type?"

You, Callie thought. *It's a type that includes exactly one person. You.*

"Oh, you know," Callie said vaguely.

"Gonna play it mysterious, huh?" Jake asked, chuckling. "Okay, that's cool. You know, it's funny, 'cause you've kind of been on my mind lately."

Stunned. Beyond stunned.

"I have?"

"Yeah. Laurel's little sister became a total fox. It's like I turned around one day and went, whoa, no more little sister."

"Oh, yeah, well, gotta be me and all that," Callie said nervously. Her hands were perspiring so much that she had to wipe them on her sweats.

"I'd really like to get to know you better, Callie," Jake said softly. "I don't really know you at all, you know. Maybe we could hang out sometime."

"Uh, sure. You mean, you and me and Laurel, right?"

"No," Jake said. "I mean you and me."

"As . . . friends, right?"

"Labels are such a drag, don't you think? Friends. What does that mean, really? Not enemies?"

"Right, right," Callie agreed quickly. "But I just meant . . . I mean, I know this is stupid but . . . well, you *are* Laurel's boyfriend."

"See? Another label. Laurel's boyfriend. Sounds lame. I'm me. And you're you. And like I just told you, I'd really like to get to know you better."

"Well, I'd like to get to know you better, too," Callie said decisively.

Her hand immediately popped over her mouth.

Did I really just say what I think I just said? To Jake Moore?

"Well, cool. Listen, I know Laurel is tied up this afternoon with some Saints thing. I was thinking we could go canoeing on one of the bayous, maybe get in a swim. You up for it?"

"Sure," Callie said, desperately casual.

"Great. I'll pick you up at two. And Callie?"

"Yuh?"

"No need to mention this to Laurel. She might misunderstand. Okay?"

"Okay. See you." Callie hung up the phone, but she couldn't move.

She went over the conversation in her mind again and again and again. Jake Moore was coming over at two o'clock to take her out. It wasn't a date. Or maybe it was. But whatever it was, it was a whole lot closer to her dream than she'd ever thought she'd get. Spending an afternoon with Jake wasn't going to hurt Laurel.

In fact, Laurel never had to know.

* * *

"I have nothing to wear!" Callie wailed.

She stood in the center of her room, surrounded by every item of clothing she had ever purchased at Threads. She finally decided on a pair of low-slung jeans that showed off her new abs and a cropped little peasant shirt. But her two bathing suits were one piece, jet black, and a million light-years from sexy.

She went down the hall to Laurel's room, went inside, and opened the middle drawer in her sister's dresser. There, neatly folded in two piles, were a half dozen bikinis—tops and bottoms.

Callie stared at them. *Like I could ever in this lifetime fit into Laurel's bikinis. Not even.*

What the heck. She fingered a really cute red- and white-gingham bikini top. The tags were still on it. Laurel hadn't worn it yet.

"Prepare for humiliation," she mumbled, pulling both halves of the bikini out of the drawer. She dropped her clothes and tried on the top.

It fit.

She slipped on the matching bottom. It fit.

She looked at her reflection in the mirror.

It couldn't be. But it was. She was wearing Laurel's bikini. And she looked every bit as cute as Laurel would in it.

There was no doubt about it. She had become a babe. And the babe was going to spend the afternoon alone with Jake Moore, the guy of her dreams. It wasn't like she was really poaching her sister's guy. They were going to be friends, that was all. But in the back of her mind, she couldn't help wonder if it could

be something more with the guy she had loved forever . . . who just happened to be Laurel's boyfriend.

Deep in thought she went to the linen closet to
pack a towel. *All's supposed to be fair in love and war,
right? And how many times did Laurel look down on me?
How many times did she act like I didn't exist? How many
times did she kiss Jake right in front of me, like I didn't have
any feelings? So what do I owe her? Nothing, that's what.*

After she dressed, she took a quick peek in her bedroom mirror. Cute. Cuter than cute. Beautiful. It was
as if somehow her dream had actually come true.

In the mirror her eyes lit on the reflection of her
Loverock. She thought about the night of the meteor,
and about wishing on the stars with Sarah and Addison. It seemed like a really, really long time ago.

A different lifetime. A different girl's life.

The doorbell rang. Jake. Downstairs, waiting for
her.

"Callie Bailey," she whispered to her reflection,
"this time you are going to be the sister who gets the
guy."

Quite simply, Callie's life changed.

Over the next two weeks she secretly hung out
with Jake three more times. He had even invited her
to sit in on a band practice one night. Pisces was great,
and Jake was so hot when he sang that Callie could
barely stand it. All they did was talk and laugh and
flirt—Jake hadn't tried to kiss her, and Callie was glad.
As long as they hadn't kissed, she could still tell herself that she wasn't doing anything so horrible.

Laurel knew nothing about it.

But whatever was going on between her and Jake, it was as if Callie Bailey, Geek Chic diva, had never existed. In her place was a confident, cool beauty. Something had happened. It wasn't so drastic that Callie wasn't still herself, yet it was so drastic that she had gone from completely forgettable to, everyone said, truly beautiful. As beautiful as Laurel.

Maybe even more beautiful than Laurel.

Her life at school was utterly different, too. She went from a girl who hung out with the geeks to a girl who hung out with everybody. One day she'd eat lunch with Addison and Sarah, the next day she'd eat with Laurel and Jake and their friends, the next day some other group.

Everyone wanted to be with Callie. It was a blast.

She told the editor of the school newspaper that "Geeks Speak" was going to go on temporary hiatus. "My heart isn't in it anymore," she informed him. "And you've got to write from your heart, right?"

The more she put Jake off, the more he seemed to want her. He was constantly finding a reason to run into her at school, to talk to her for a few minutes when he called to talk to Laurel, and to show up at the Baileys' when he knew that Laurel was out.

The power made Callie giddy.

So *this* was what it was like to be beautiful. However great she had thought it would be, it was even better. It was everything.

Soon, she thought one day, after she'd just gotten off the phone with a very flirtatious, very eager Jake, *soon I will let him kiss me. And that kiss will be the final nail in the coffin of Laurel-and-Jake.*

All Callie could think was: it's about time.

Addison walked Callie home after school that Friday as he always did. They talked about the stuff they always talked about—movies and music and the insipidness of high school. But his mind was someplace else.

As far as he was concerned, Callie had always been beautiful. Perfect, in fact. But now she was a different kind of beautiful. It was, frankly, dazzling. And kind of intimidating. He wasn't sure if he liked it or not. But there was no doubt in his mind that he was more in love with her than ever.

Ever since the night of Leesa's party he'd been trying to screw up his courage to ask her out on an actual date. But the better looking she got, the more difficult it was. It was like he couldn't get the words formed in his mouth. He had practiced just what he would say to her in front of his mirror many times.

But every time he was with her, the words stuck in his throat.

The Dave Matthews Band concert had come and gone. Blown opportunity there, huh? So now he was thinking about something much more casual. He'd invite her over to his house, they'd rent some classic films, and then, after they were both in a really great, laid-back mood, he'd tell her how he really felt about her.

All he had to do was ask her over. Offhand. Casual. He could do it.

They got to the walkway that led up to Callie's house, and Addison told himself that now was the time, but he felt as if his tongue was Superglued to the roof of his mouth.

"Wanna come in for a snack?" Callie asked him. "I think my mom actually baked something."

Addison shook his head. "My mom's getting home late from work tonight. I get to make dinner, big joy."

"My advice is, nuke a package," Callie said. "So, listen, call me tonight, I'm not doing anything. Plus I really want to check my trig against yours." She leaned over to give him a friendly kiss on the cheek.

It was now or never, he figured.

Deep breath, Addison. Go for it.

"So, Cal, listen. Do you have plans for Sunday? Like late in the afternoon?"

She shrugged. "I don't think so, why?"

"Wanna come over and rent some vids? Order a pizza or something?"

Callie thought for moment. She didn't have anything planned with Jake for Sunday. No secret rendezvous.

"Sure," she told Addison. "Sounds like fun."

"It does? I mean, it does!" Addison said quickly. "So, that's great then. Four o'clock?"

"Yeah, sure. See ya." She waved to him as she headed into the house.

Addison was so happy that he punched the air. It was going to happen. Him and Callie. Was life great, or what?

Callie dumped her backpack on the table in the

hallway, then immediately checked the answering machine. Lately, she got as many phone calls as Laurel did.

One message. Callie pushed the Play button.

"Hi?" the voice said. "This is Ashlee Raines, down at Threads? For Laurel?"

Ashlee is one of those girls, Callie thought, with a wry smile, *who turns every sentence into a question when she talks on the phone.*

"So, Laurel, there's an emergency down here at Threads? And this big photographer came in from Houston to take some pictures for a window display? And the model that was booked, like, ran away and eloped with her boyfriend or something? So we were wondering if you could, like, fill in this afternoon? I know it's last minute, but the pay is two-fifty for two hours? So call us right away, okay?"

She left the number, and the message ended.

Two-fifty for two hours, Callie thought. As in two hundred and fifty dollars. Amazing. Just because Laurel is beautiful enough that a photographer would want to—

Callie couldn't even finish the thought.

Because another thought had taken its place.

She was as beautiful as Laurel now. Everyone said so. They wore the same size. And Laurel had a Saints meeting, and then she was going over to Julia Birch's house to study.

What a shame. There was no way that she could do the gig for Threads.

Callie picked up the phone and dialed Threads.

"Threads, may I help you?" someone answered.

"May I speak with Ashlee, please?"

"This is Ashlee?"

"Oh, hi, this is Laurel Bailey's sister, Callie. Look, I just got home and heard your message about the photo shoot. But Laurel's all tied up, so she can't make it."

"Darn," Ashlee said, "because she would have been, you know, perfect?"

"You know, Laurel and I wear exactly the same size now," Callie said casually. "A photographer is taking some portfolio modeling shots of me next week."

"Oh, my gosh, isn't this a great idea? How about if maybe you do the shoot?" Ashlee asked. "I'd love to do it myself, but the company has a rule that employees can't model? So could you, like buzz by here and let the photographer take a look at you?"

Callie's heart pounded like a drum. "Um, let me think about it for a sec . . . well, I don't really want to make a career of it, Ashlee, but you were so nice to me when I came in the other day."

"You're such a sweetheart to do this, okay?" Ashlee said. "I really think he'll want to use you when he sees you, you know?"

Callie hung up and a smile spread across her face.

Callie Bailey, model.

She liked the sound of that. A lot.

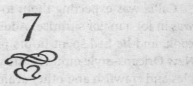

Chapter 7

*T*oday, Addison thought, *is the day my life changes. No more Addison, best bud. Ladies and gentlemen, meet Addison, boyfriend.*

He looked around his basement rec room, normally a disorganized mess of family flotsam. However, with a lot of hard work—he'd slaved all morning and most of the afternoon—he had single-handedly transformed it into a den of romance.

All the junk that usually filled the room was now in the storage space under the stairs. There were vases and glasses everywhere filled with fresh flowers that he'd picked in the park across from his house. He'd vacuumed the rug, waxed the furniture, and scrubbed the old crayon marks off the walls. Then he'd covered the ratty sofa with a lace tablecloth. He put fat little candles in small dishes and set them around the room.

And then, as a last touch, he burned jasmine incense around two-thirty—just enough to add a lingering touch of scent to the room at four.

But the pièce de résistance was in the oven.

Callie was expecting them to order in pizza, so she was in for a major surprise. Addison was a pretty good cook, and he had spent hours preparing an authentic New Orleans–style étouffée: steaming rice and vegetables and crawfish and other seafood, together with exotic spices he had picked up at a local Cajun market.

The étouffée would be ready, he figured, just in time for the end of the first movie. Then they'd eat, and then they'd watch the second one. He'd picked the films carefully, thinking about what Callie especially enjoyed. He'd selected two classics about classic outsiders, Jack Nicholson in *One Flew Over the Cuckoo's Nest* and James Dean in *Rebel Without a Cause*.

Okay, so they'd eat. And then, before he turned on the second movie, out would come his final great romantic surprise—*Callie and Addison: The Video.*

Addison had spent many hours secretly working on it in the school video lab. He felt sure this video was the perfect way to let her know how he really felt.

— He paced the room nervously, thinking that Callie was going to be so surprised when she saw that he wasn't wearing outfits 1, 2, or 3. His shirt was entirely new. The salesgirl at The Gap said it made him look like Ryan Phillippe, so he bought it even though it meant using some of the money he'd been saving for Christmas.

Well, he'd worry about that later.

Addison checked his watch. Eight minutes before Callie was due to arrive. She was never early. *Callie and Addison: The Video* was only five minutes long. So he had plenty of time to watch it and rewind before she arrived.

It would give him something to do besides sweat.

He popped the video into the VCR, then sat on the lace-covered couch as it started to roll.

The theme music from *Dawson's Creek* came up on the screen, along with a still photo of Callie and Addison from nursery school. She had her hands on her hips and was scowling at the camera. He had his arm around her, a look of utter happiness on his face. More pictures of the two of them together— the first-grade nutrition pageant, with her dressed as a tomato and him dressed as a carrot; them competing in a wheelbarrow race at the fourth-grade Olympics; a summer fishing trip at age eleven when Callie had hooked a huge catfish; even a photo of them dancing at the party after Jenny Sheppard's bat mitzvah.

Addison literally felt a lump in his throat as he watched this chronicle of their lives together.

But the best of the video was yet to come.

As the music continued to play, the video shifted from stills to moving pictures. Addison had copied clips of some very romantic moments from his and Callie's favorite television shows, past and present, and strung them together: *Dawson's Creek,* of course, but also *Party of Five* and *The Wonder Years* and even a couple from *The Love Boat* and *Love Connection,* which they both loved because the shows were just so cheesy.

The sequence ended with the image of Dawson and Joey together, down by the creek, their arms around each other, staring soulfully into each other's eyes.

And then, as the music faded out, Addison cross-faded from that scene to a shot of him, Addison, sitting on a swing at the same nursery school they had attended.

"It's funny," Addison heard himself say on the video, "that sometimes, when you know someone so well, you don't see what's right in front of your face. And you won't let yourself feel in your heart what you really feel for them. That's Addison and Callie."

The video ran out with the same theme music playing and a long shot of the sun setting over the bayou.

Addison sighed. It was going to take a lot of guts to show that video to Callie. But he'd made his decision. He was going to do it. Definitely.

He rewound the video and went to turn down the heat on the étouffée. He straightened a few things in the room that didn't need straightening, rearranged a few flowers that didn't need rearranging, and looked at his watch again.

Five minutes after the hour.

It was show time.

Callie stuck her hair up in a messy bun. After all, she was only going to Addison's. She pulled on a T-shirt and was just zipping her jeans when the phone rang.

"Hello?"

"Callie, it's Jake."

Jake. His voice always sent little chills of pleasure down her spine.

"Hi," she said softly, reaching down to pet Jumby, the family cat.

"Listen, I am so bummed. You know Derrick, my drummer? The guy thinks he's a songwriter, right? So he just pulled this major freak-out because I told him we won't do any of his tunes. Basically, he walked. And we've got a big gig next Saturday."

"That's terrible," Callie sympathized.

"Tell me. The guy's a great drummer. If he walks, there's no way I can—listen, I really need to talk to you, Callie. Can I come over?"

She checked her watch. She had an hour before she was due at Addison's, and since she was never on time, he wouldn't really expect her until four-thirty. And all they were going to do was watch videos, so it was no biggie to be on time. Plus, she knew for sure that her parents were spending the afternoon and evening in the city and Laurel had gone shopping with some of the girls from The Saints. Which meant she had the house to herself.

Undoubtedly, Jake already knew that Laurel was out.

"Sure, come on," Callie agreed. "But you can't stay long because I have plans later."

"Male or female?" Jake asked sharply.

"See you soon," Callie said coyly. Then she hung up. She had Jake Moore right where she wanted him. He was actually jealous!

She quickly rearranged her hair—a messy bun was fine for Addison, but this was *Jake*—spritzed on some perfume, put on some light makeup, and headed downstairs. Then she got out some iced tea and glasses and left a note on the front door instructing him to come to the back porch.

Five minutes later he arrived, looking perfect as always. She'd been in love with him for so many years, had dreamed about him seeing her and wanting her, and now it was really happening. There he was.

Gazing at her as if she was the most beautiful girl in the world.

She handed him a glass of iced tea, but he put the tea on the table next to him and sat down next to her on the glider.

"You are something else," he murmured.

"What does that mean?"

Jake chuckled and shook his head.

"So, what's up with your drummer?" Callie asked.

"What is it about you, Callie? I can't stop thinking about you." He laughed again. "What did you do, put some kind of a spell on me?"

"Yep," Callie said lightly. "It's the voodoo, man," she added in her spookiest voice.

He reached out and smoothed some hair off her face. "What'd you do, make one of those little dolls of me and stick pins in it?"

"If I did that, you'd be in pain," Callie teased. "And you're not in pain. Are you?"

"Yeah," he whispered huskily. "And you know it." He leaned toward her.

She deftly moved away, picked up her tea, and took a sip. "So, what's the deal with Derrick? Isn't that why you wanted to come over?"

"Actually, we settled that."

"You settled it?"

"Yeah. Between the time I called you and the time I got here, Derrick saw the light. I guess he remembered that we're getting paid for that gig Saturday night." He reached for her hand. "You'll come, won't you?"

She took her hand back. "What about Laurel?"

"What about her?"

"You guys are still a couple. Right?"

Jake scratched his chin. "It's kind of over."

"But you're still seeing her," Callie commented. "I know that the phone rings for her. And you're the one calling."

"And she thinks you and I are just friends," Jake said, nodding. "Very understanding of her, really. But I'm just kind of looking for the right time to—you know. Look, Callie, things change. Laurel just doesn't . . . she doesn't do it for me anymore. Everything's so by-the-book with her, you know? Hang with the right people, wear the right clothes, rule the school. It's all so predictable. That stuff is utterly unimportant to me."

"So, what's important, then?"

"My music." He stared at her. "You."

"Not Laurel?"

He shook his head no.

"But . . . Laurel doesn't know that."

"Right."

"What are you going to tell her?" Callie whispered.

"The truth. That we didn't plan this, it just happened," Jake said.

Callie nodded. She knew that was a lie. Maybe Jake hadn't planned this, but she sure had. They were both sneaking around behind Laurel's back—and it was wrong, terrible, disloyal, and—

Whatever. Callie didn't care. Beautiful, perfect Laurel had always gotten every single thing she had ever wanted. She could get the next thing she wanted, too. She had no idea what it was like to be Callie, and always compared to a gorgeous sister. She didn't know what it was like to want a guy so much, for so many years, that you lay in bed at night with tears tracking down the sides of your face, because you knew that never, ever in a million years was he going to see you as a girl he could want, a girl he could love.

Yet the impossible had happened. Surely, just this once, Callie deserved to have it all.

"Jake," she whispered. Callie closed her eyes as he brought one hand to her cheek. His lips came down on hers in the softest, sweetest, sexiest kiss in the world.

"Oh, Callie," he whispered back. "Oh, Callie."

Addison couldn't believe it. He checked his watch against the clock on the wall for the zillionth time. Six o'clock. Callie had a bad habit of showing up late, yes, but never *this* late, not without a phone call to explain.

At four forty-five, he'd finally called her. But there had been no answer and he'd just left some lame message on the answering machine. He'd called again at five. And at five-thirty. And he'd called again just five minutes ago. He'd said for her to call him right away because he was really getting worried about her.

No call. No Callie.

The étouffée had turned into cat food long ago. The jasmine incense had been overpowered by the aroma of overcooked étouffée. The fragile wildflowers had wilted in their vases. The cat had broken one of these vases, and pieces of it, flower petals, and a pool of water made a sad little still life in the corner.

Addison was too depressed to clean it up.

How could Callie do this to him?

And then it dawned on him. She couldn't. No possible way. Which could only mean one thing. It was like a fist in his gut: Callie had been in some horrible accident. It was the only explanation that made sense.

He picked up the phone and punched her number in one more time, hoping against hope . . .

No answer except the answering machine.

Addison sat there, his hands dangling between his knees. If anything had happened to Callie—

It was too horrible to think about.

He had to go look for her. Find her. Save her.

He took the basement stairs two at a time and ran toward the Baileys' house. A chant began inside his head, that matched every jogging step as his feet hit the pavement: please-let-her-be-okay-please-she-has-to-be-okay.

Over and over and over.

Wherever you are, Callie, whatever happened, hold on. I'm coming.

Kissing Jake, cuddled up in his strong arms, the feel of his hand stroking her hair. It was bliss. Sometimes they would talk. Or rather, Jake would talk. About his band. And how much his music meant to him. And how lame it was in St. Charles, boring burb of New Orleans, and how he was going to make it as a rock star one way or another.

Even listening to Jake was thrilling. Because he wasn't telling Laurel, he was telling her, Callie. And Saturday night, when Pisces played in New Orleans, Callie would be the girl in the audience who belonged with Jake. Callie would be the girl all the other girls would envy.

After another fantastic kiss, it was Jake who finally checked his watch. "Wow, time flies and all that. We'd better take this show on the road, 'cuz your sister could walk in any minute."

He got up and reached down to pull her up, but Callie was checking her own watch.

"Oh, my God," she said, jumping up. "I completely lost track of time. I am so, so late."

"But I thought we might cruise out to the park, do some duck gazing. Some Callie gazing—"

"I can't. Oh, my gosh, I can't believe it's dark. I was supposed to be at Addison's hours ago."

"The geek? Call him and blow him off."

"No, I can't. I really have to go."

He slipped his arms around her waist. "Come on. What were you two gonna do, work on his stamp collection? Call him and say something came up."

Callie shook her head. "Besides, you need to talk to Laurel before we . . . spend any more time together. Don't you think?"

"Yeah, you're right. Okay. One last kiss and I'm outta here, and so are you."

He pulled her to him.

She never saw Addison come running around the side of the house, never saw him come to a shocked stop at the side of the back porch.

He stared at Callie. She was in Jake's arms. Jake. Her sister's boyfriend. It didn't seem real, but it was. Laurel's boyfriend and Callie, locked in an embrace, starkly illuminated by the porch light.

"Callie?" Her name slipped out of Addison's mouth before he even realized he'd said it.

Callie opened her eyes and saw him. "Addison?"

For a long moment Addison froze. And then he did the only thing he could—he ran away.

"Addison!" Callie called after him. "Addison, please, come back!"

"Leave me alone!" he yelled over his shoulder. He kept running, as if somehow, if he ran fast enough and far enough, he could make the terrible thing he had just seen not be true.

Chapter
8

There he was. By his locker, getting his stuff together for Mr. Livelli's class.

Callie had looked for Addison all day long. After he'd run away the night before, she heard on her answering machine how may times he'd tried to call her. She felt badly that he'd been worried about her.

Still, she had two parents, and Addison wasn't one of them.

But Addison was her buddy, and she wanted to make things right between them. So she'd called him three times Sunday night. No answer.

He didn't make it to homeroom. He hadn't made it to trig, either, so she wondered if he was sick. But Addison never got sick. So she'd borrowed Alexis's cell phone between classes and tried him again, but still there was no answer.

Just when she was sure he'd run away to New York to write plays, there he was, his usual geeky self, wearing Outfit #2.

"Hi," she said, walking up to him. "I was starting to think you were ignoring me."

He gave her a killer look and took another book from his locker.

"Okay, well, this just shows how perceptive I am," Callie went on. "You *are* ignoring me."

"Why would I do something like that?"

"That's what I'm trying to find out," Callie said. "I thought you'd be happy to see me. Silly me."

He gave a short, dark laugh and slammed his locker shut. "You thought I'd be happy? Interesting."

Callie shook her perfect hair off her face. "I've been looking for you all day. To apologize."

"Gee," Addison drawled, "if I'd known that, I'd have fallen to the floor in gratitude. Perhaps while down there, I could give your extremely hip new shoes a spit shine."

"What is your prob—"

Callie was drowned out by a group of kids who ran down the hall screaming about how they were going to beat Northside High School on Friday night. Addison took the opportunity to get going.

Callie couldn't believe he was walking away from her. She hurried after him.

"What is wrong with you?" she asked.

"With me? Nothing," Addison said and sped up.

She trotted alongside him. "Okay, you're really, really upset about last night, is that it?"

"I'm upset about ongoing human rights abuses in the former Yugoslavia," Addison said. "I'm upset that people wear the fur of animals that are tortured for their pelts. I'm upset by racism, sexism, and homophobia. But last night? Last night is barely a blip on the screen of my life, Callie. So don't flatter yourself."

"Look, Addison, I know I should have called," Callie said. "I meant to, but—"

They were outside the door to Livelli's room. Addison stopped suddenly and whirled around. "You *meant* to? Oh, well, in that case, never mind. As long as you *meant* to."

"Why are you making such a big deal about this?"

"Why?" Addison seethed. "Let's try because when you were two and a half hours late, I got a little worried, Callie. I pictured you dead in a ditch somewhere—"

"That's a little melodramatic—"

"Gee, I don't think so. I went out looking for you because I knew you would never not call unless something really terrible had happened. So I ran to your house. And there you were, swapping spit with Jake Moore!"

"Yo, calm down, geek-boy!" Jim Kagen hooted as he sauntered into class with Alexis. "I know Callie's hot, but don't let her give you a geekified heart attack."

"Get outta my face," Addison snapped.

"Addison, listen," Callie began. "I—"

Sarah Brown walked over to them. "Hey, you guys, I hear Livelli went home sick and they called a sub who isn't here . . ." she started to say, and then took in the angry expressions on their faces. "Never mind." She tiptoed into class.

"Look," Callie began again. "I should have called. I'm sorry. But I don't know what the big deal is—"

"You don't." Addison's chin jutted out. His eyes clouded with hurt. "It was a really big deal, Callie. I had cooked dinner for you. I had this big surprise planned—"

"But it was just supposed to be videos and—"

"What difference does that make? What, if it was just Addison and videos, then no biggie, I can stand him up? Show up when I feel like it? Not show up at all? Because I'm much too busy making out with my *sister's boyfriend?* What do you call that, Callie?"

"It's not what it looked like—"

Addison laughed derisively. "Sure. It was Truth or Dare. No, wait. Someone forced you to stand me up, stay home, and get down with your sister's boyfriend—"

"He's not my sister's boyfriend!" Callie yelled.

Addison eyed her cynically.

Callie sighed. "He's my boyfriend, Addison."

Addison blinked and pushed his glasses up his nose. "You wanna run that little wrinkle by me again?"

"He's my *boyfriend*," Callie repeated.

"Have you two bothered to tell Laurel? Or is she just as much in the dark as I was?"

"Jake's going to tell her. Soon."

"Soon," Addison echoed. "You were making out

with Jake, who Laurel still thinks is her boyfriend, but Jake is gonna tell her *soon*. Callie, do you hear yourself?"

"Look, I was getting ready to come over to your house when Jake called me. He was all upset about something that happened with his band," Callie explained. "He asked if he could stop over, and I thought it would just be a few minutes, and . . . well, we lost track of time. Jake and I . . . it just happened. We didn't plan it."

"You know what you sound like?" Addison asked. "A bad talk show."

"Because I didn't understand—"

"No one with any feelings or character or anything that remotely resembles ethics could ever—"

"Fine, Addison. Trash me," Callie said stiffly. "You're supposed to be my bud. You're supposed to be happy for me. You don't understand because you've never been in love."

Addison smiled sadly. "You know who you are, Callie? The blindest person in Louisiana. And I am, without a doubt, the biggest idiot."

"Why?" Callie asked, both concerned and confused.

"See if you can figure out the punch line to this joke, Callie. What geek guy was totally in love with what former Geek Chic diva?"

Callie's jaw dropped open.

"I know, so funny you forgot to laugh," Addison said bitterly.

"But—but—I had no idea," Callie stammered.

"Of course not. You were too busy crunching your Abs of Steel and finding perfect lipstick and stealing your sister's boyfriend. I don't even know who you are anymore."

"I'm me," Callie insisted. "Just because I got better looking—"

"On the outside, maybe, in some plastic way," Addison said. "But your kind of ugly is ugly to the bone."

Callie gulped hard. "Okay. You wanted to hurt me, you hurt me. Happy now?"

"Not really," Addison said. "But for now, cheap, petty revenge will have to do. The good news for me is that the real Callie Bailey, the girl I loved, doesn't exist anymore. For all I know, she never did. So there's no chance she'll break my heart again."

With one last cold look, he walked past her into the classroom. Everyone was in party mode, awaiting the sub. Callie hurried after him and touched his shoulder.

"Addison, wait." He turned to her.

"You're still my friend," she insisted. "My best friend."

"You don't know the meaning of the word, Callie," Addison said sadly. "As of right now, our friendship is officially over."

A week later Callie and Jake were sitting side by side on the couch in the luxurious waiting room of Bleu Bayou Model and Talent modeling agency. The wall were covered with ads, head shots and full-length shots, all of gorgeous models represented by Bleu Bayou.

Callie was about to join the agency.

Bleu Bayou had set up the emergency shoot at Threads. Since then, Callie had done two more fill-in jobs for them. She'd also intercepted a message that had been left for Laurel about modeling at a fashion show for a very upscale boutique. Callie had secured that job the same way she'd gotten the Threads job: Laurel never heard about it.

Just the other evening at dinner, Laurel mentioned that she hadn't gotten any modeling calls lately, and Callie shrugged. Inside, though, she couldn't help but feel a little thrill of triumph.

Yesterday, Geneva Toups from Bleu Bayou had called Callie. The photographer from the Threads shoot thought Callie was sensational. Would Callie like to come in and talk about signing with the agency?

Would she? Bleu Bayou was the most prestigious agency in New Orleans. Laurel freelanced for them sometimes, but they'd never expressed any interest in signing her.

This all was so exciting that it almost made up for her huge fight with Addison. Almost, but not quite. Callie couldn't believe that Addison really was putting an end to their friendship. It didn't seem possible. As for the love thing . . . well, she'd never given him any reason to think they were romantically involved.

If he'd imagined something that didn't exist, he couldn't very well get mad at her for it.

Jake played with a lock of her hair. "So, you ready to fly off to Hollywood and become a star?"

"I'm ready to make money," Callie replied.

"You could be a star, you know," Jake said. "You have the looks for it. And the fire."

"Don't." She pushed his hand away from her hair. "It has to look perfect when I go in."

"Trust me," Jake said, "it does."

Jake had driven Callie into downtown New Orleans. He'd insisted, in fact, on being there for the moment of the big signing.

"Jake?"

"Hmmm?"

"When are you going to talk to Laurel?"

"Soon."

"How soon?"

Jake leaned back. "It's not so easy. I don't want to hurt her."

"But it *will* hurt her," Callie pointed out. "And the longer we sneak around behind her back, the more hurt she'll be."

"She doesn't suspect a thing, Callie. I've been extra nice to her. I just don't think we should rush this. Laurel has a college visit to Emory in a couple of days. You know how nervous she is about it. You think it would be fair to tell her now?"

"When, then?" Callie pressed.

"Soon," Jake promised. "I promise."

An interior door opened, and a tall, slender woman who appeared to be in her forties walked briskly over to them. Callie and Jake stood to meet her.

"Callie, Geneva Toups." She held out her hand.

"Nice to meet you," Callie said, shaking hands with her. "Oh, this is my boyfriend, Jake Moore."

Geneva smiled at him. "You could probably make some money in our men's division, Jake."

"No, thanks." Jake grinned. "I'll stick with music."

"Let me know if you change your mind. Well, Callie, please come into my office so we can chat. Excuse us, won't you, Jake?"

Geneva's office was done in shades of white and off-white, with an eggshell-colored velvet couch covered in off-white silk and satin pillows. There was a panoramic view of New Orleans through her floor-to-ceiling windows.

"Wow, this is amazing," Callie said breathily.

"Yes, it is nice," Geneva agreed. "Please, have a seat. Can we bring you anything? Bottled water? Coffee?"

"No, I'm fine, thank you." Callie sat on the velvet couch. She was nervous—all of this was so new to her. She only hoped that her outfit of khakis and a white cashmere sweater that she'd borrowed from Laurel—without permission—was the right look.

Geneva sat behind her imposing desk. "I'll be direct, though it runs counter to all my southern breeding," Geneva told Callie, and flashed her a quick smile. "But I'm a busy woman and this has been an exceptionally busy day."

"Fine," Callie said politely.

Geneva opened a manila folder that had been on her desk. There were various 8" × 10" photos of Callie from her shoot for Threads, plus some other shots the photographer had taken just for fun: close-ups, Callie goofing around with soap bubbles and a wand, Callie getting a bouquet of flowers from a little boy who was in the store with his mom.

"Everyone loves the Threads shoot," she told Callie. "It turned out better than if Laurel had been our model."

Callie smiled. "That's a real compliment, thank you."

"You're welcome. But even better were the shots Phil did afterward. . . ." She looked at the photo of the little boy handing Callie the flowers. "Dynamite."

"Well, thank you again," Callie said.

"No need to thank me, Callie. I wouldn't say it if it wasn't true," Geneva said briskly. "Let me cut to the chase. You aren't as tall as Laurel. That limits you somewhat for high fashion. Some clients care, others don't. But for commercial work—"

"I'm sorry. What's that?" Callie interrupted.

Geneva laughed. "You are a rookie, aren't you? That's all right. Nothing this business loves more than a fresh, new face. Commercial work is everything other than fashion. TV commercials, cosmetics, perfume, product ads for magazines, billboards, et cetera."

"Wow," Callie exclaimed.

"Wow is right. Just from these pictures, I've set you up with ten go-sees—that means going to see the client about the booking—plus a couple of confirmed gigs. I think you have a major future with us, Callie. We'd like to sign you." She pushed a contract toward Callie.

Callie reached over and picked it up.

"It's quite standard. We take fifteen percent and you can't book except through us," Geneva explained.

"But my sister freelances," Callie pointed out.

Geneva nodded. "Your sister is lovely. But her type is much more common than yours, which is why we've never signed her. It's a dog-eat-dog business, I'm afraid. Frankly, if Laurel had told us about you, you could have been working for us for at least two years, already."

Callie shrugged. "Maybe she was protecting her turf."

Geneva sighed and made a tent with her fingers. "I have to tell you, Callie, some of the bookings you're being considered for are things that Laurel might have done. But as I said, your look is simply more unique. And fresh. And . . ." Geneva shrugged. "This is a business. It's all about the bottom line. You're an exciting fresh face, Callie. I think you can be quite successful with us."

She stood up and came around her desk. Callie stood up, too. "Thank you, Ms. Toups."

"Please, Geneva," the older woman insisted. "You're a minor, so your parents will need to okay this. Show it to the family lawyer if you like. But I'd like it signed, sealed, and delivered within the next week or so. Meanwhile, I'll trust you enough to send you out on these go-sees, starting tomorrow." She handed Callie a list.

"Thank you again, Geneva."

The older woman walked her to the door. "I'll talk with you soon, Callie. I think you're going to make both of us a lot of money."

Callie floated back to the waiting room. The gorgeous receptionist waved at Callie and said, "Welcome to Bleu Bayou, Sweetie!" Jake rose when he saw her.

"How'd it go?" he asked.

Callie's answer was a big smile and a running leap into his strong arms. "I'm in!" she screamed. He twirled her around in a circle. She'd seen him do that with Laurel so many times.

Only now it was her in his arms. And he was hers. It was *all* hers. "Kiss me," she said breathlessly. "Now."

Jake obliged.

Behind them, someone cried out.

They broke apart. Laurel. She'd just come in the door. Tears were streaming down her cheeks.

"Laurel—" Callie began. But then she had no idea what to say. She looked over at Jake, but he just stood there, an idiotic expression on his face.

"How *could* you?" Laurel hissed. She punched Jake in the arm as hard as she could. "I *hate* you!"

"We didn't plan this, Laurel," Jake said. "We never meant to hurt you. It just happened."

Callie winced at how empty that sounded, how dumb. She felt the eyes of the receptionist on them, greedily taking it all in.

Laurel stood in front of her, vibrating with rage. "I got a call from Grace's Boutique today. They were sorry I hadn't been available for their fashion show. The fashion show that *you* did, they told me. Then I ran into Ashlee from Threads. Guess the rest."

Callie's cheeks burned with embarrassment, but she held her head high. Years of pent-up resentment bubbled to the surface. "I guess you never thought about offering to help me get into modeling, did you?"

"All you had to do was ask, Callie," Laurel said. "But instead, you stole my jobs. You stole my modeling agency. And then you stole my boyfriend."

Callie gave her sister a cold look. "I didn't steal him. You lost him. So I guess there wasn't very much there to begin with."

"Things change, Laurel," Jake said. "That's life."

"Shut up, jerk," Laurel snapped viciously.

Callie came so close to Laurel that she almost whispered in her ear. "It hurts to be the sister who loses? I know it's a new experience for you. But look at it this way: now you know how I felt. All those years. And you never even noticed. Callie the geek."

"That wasn't my fault!" Laurel cried.

"Never as good, never as pretty, never as *anything*," Callie hissed. "Well, now I'm *everything*. Deal with it."

Laurel's eyes met Callie's. Then she pulled her hand back and slapped her sister's cheek as hard as she could.

And then she ran out the door.

"Wow, that was trashy!" the receptionist marveled.

"Nice shot," Callie said ruefully, touching her hand to her bright-red cheek.

"You okay?" Jake asked. "Listen, do you think we should go after her?"

"What for?" Callie asked. "She's ticked off, but she'll live."

"I have a bad feeling about this."

Now that Callie was getting over the slap, she did,

too. "Laurel's too sane to do anything terrible," she insisted, more to convince herself than to convince Jake.

They stared at each other, hesitating. Then, as if by unspoken agreement, they hurried out the door. But by the time they got downstairs, Laurel's little red Miata was already peeling off into the traffic.

Chapter

9

"*T*here! Laurel's Miata!" Callie pointed as they rounded a curve in the road. The light at the next intersection turned amber and Laurel slipped through, but Jake was caught by the red light.

The extremely long red light.

By the time the light changed, the Miata was nowhere to be seen. Jake followed the signs to the interstate and got on, hoping against hope that they would see Laurel's car.

No luck.

Inside Jake's car, Callie and he were utterly silent.

"She'll get over this," Jake finally said. "She's just jealous about the modeling thing. And about her and me—well, people break up all the time."

Callie sighed and leaned her head back against the headrest. *It's just as well we didn't catch Laurel*, she thought. *Because if we had, I have no idea what I would have said.*

Jake pulled his Jeep into Callie's driveway. Laurel's car wasn't there. He turned to Callie. "So, you okay?"

"Yeah, I guess."

"Hey, I'll take you out to dinner this weekend, and we'll celebrate your modeling contract, okay?"

Callie nodded, but her heart wasn't in it.

"Cheer up, beautiful," Jake said, reaching for her. "You're young, gorgeous, and about to sign with a hot modeling agency. Your sister's tweaked 'cuz something rocked her little world. It'll probably do her good." He leaned over and kissed her. "I'll be at band practice 'til, like ten, but I'll call you when I get home."

Callie let herself into the pitch-black house—obviously no one was home. She was going to have to show her parents the modeling contract when they got back from her father's sales conference in Chicago. And they were going to have to find out everything that had happened with Laurel.

They're going to be disappointed in me, Callie thought as she trudged upstairs. *But they don't understand what it was like to be me before I got cute. Neither does Laurel. Jake is right. Laurel will get over this. It's not really that big a deal. I mean, I was madly in love with Jake way before he and Laurel were even a couple. Laurel will be with some other guy by tomorrow.*

Callie managed to convince herself that everything would work out and that she hadn't done anything so terrible. So what if one little bad thing had happened to perfect Little Miss Everything? Jake was right—it would probably do her sister good.

When they'd pulled into the driveway, neither she nor Jake had seen the black sedan that had been discreetly parked across the street.

She had no idea that she was being watched by people very, very interested in the changes going on in her life.

Sines. Cosines. Callie stared at her trig book as equations swam before her eyes. She'd been trying to do her homework for forty-five minutes, but all she could think about was her sister. One part of her wished Laurel would walk in the door so that Callie would know she was okay and so that they could get their big fight over. Another part hoped Laurel would spend the night with Leesa or Julia so that Callie wouldn't have to deal with her until the next day.

Homework was hopeless. Callie got up and went through her closet, taking out everything that belonged to Laurel. Maybe returning Laurel's stuff would help lessen her guilt. Funny. Laurel had never said a single word about all the stuff Callie "borrowed." But she was far too meticulous a person not to realize that stuff was missing.

I bet she knew I was borrowing her clothes but just didn't say anything, Callie thought, momentarily guilty. *Well, most sisters would be happy to lend their clothes to their younger sister.*

After that she went down to the family room and turned on the TV. She vegged out in front of *Change of Heart*, where a couple who was having problems went on arranged blind dates and then decided whether or not to stay with their current boyfriend or girlfriend.

Callie scrutinized the girl talking about her arranged date: *Frizzy hair, thunder thighs, seriously out of shape, outfit by Thrifty Mart. What a geek.*

The phone rang. Callie hoped it wasn't Laurel. Or Addison. Or Sarah.

Why are so many people stressing me? Callie thought irritably. *Why can't they just accept the fact that I'm not a geek girl they can kick around anymore?*

She reached for the phone on the coffee table. "Hello?"

"Hello," a businesslike female voice said. "Is this the Bailey residence?"

"Yes," Callie said.

"May I speak with either Mr. or Mrs. Bailey, please."

Someone selling something, Laurel thought.

"They're not home right now," Callie said. "And whatever it is you're selling, they're not—"

"This is not a sales call. When do you expect Mr. or Mrs. Bailey to return?"

"If this isn't a sales call, then what is it?" Callie snapped. She was in no mood to play games.

"This is Ms. Arthur in the admitting office at St. Charles Regional Medical Center. To whom am I speaking?"

Dread filled her. "This is Callie Bailey," she said, her voice now meek.

"Are you a relative of Miss Laurel Elizabeth Bailey?"

"She's my sister," Callie said. It came out as a whisper. "Did something happen?"

"Do you have a number where your parents can be reached, miss?" the woman said.

"Tell me what happened to my sister!" Callie demanded.

"Miss, I need the—"

"My parents are in Chicago!" Callie screamed. "Now, tell me what happened to my sister!"

"Your sister Laurel was in an accident," Ms. Arthur said.

"No. Please, no . . ."

"I will need the number of where your parents are staying in—"

Callie threw the phone down.

No, no, no, this can't be happening, Callie thought as she raced upstairs and started frantically tearing through the papers on her desk. Buried somewhere under the mess was a student directory at St. Charles Parish Regional High School, and somewhere in that directory was the number of Donald Zuckerman, the bass player in Jake's band. Pisces was rehearsing at Donald's house.

She flung papers on the floor, frantically digging through the mess that she always meant to organize but never did.

Please, Laurel, please, you have to be all right.

She kept digging. Nothing. She raced into Laurel's room and found a school directory on the corner of Laurel's perfectly neat desk. Quickly she looked up Donald's number and punched the digits into Laurel's phone. She paced as the phone rang and rang and rang. If the band was practicing, they wouldn't be able to hear the phone, or they wouldn't stop to answer it, or—

"Yeah?" a male voice barked into the phone.

"Donald, it's Callie Bailey," Callie said quickly. "I need to speak with Jake."

"Yeah, well, he's kinda busy."

"Well, it's kinda an emergency."

"He's in the middle of a major fight with our jerk of a drummer," Donald said. "You'll have to call—"

"Get him this minute, or I will personally separate your head from your neck."

"Control freak," Donald muttered. "Yo, Jake! Your lady is on the phone, man."

Callie couldn't hear what Jake said to him, but she heard Donald's reply. "I already told her you were busy, but she's, like, all tweaked about something."

Callie waited. And waited. Finally Jake got on.

"Yeah, what's up?" he said tersely. "I'm in the middle of one awful practice."

"Laurel was in an accident," Callie said. "The hospital just called me. You have to come get me and take me over there, Jake."

"Whoa. Is she okay?"

"I have no idea, just get over here."

"But what happened?" Jake asked.

"Look, I just said I don't know. Some woman from St. Charles Regional called. My parents are in Chicago, and I have to get to the hospital, so just hang up and come and get me."

Silence.

"Jake? Did you hear me?"

"Yeah, just a sec."

Callie heard someone in the background. "Hey, if Jake's ego can't even take the comp, then—"

"Jake, you'd better get in here, man!" someone else yelled.

"Jake!"

"Yeah," Jake said into the phone. "Look, Callie, it's hitting the fan here. It's a really bad time—"

"Didn't you hear me?" Callie cried. "We have to get to the hospital."

"Yo, Jake?" someone called.

"Yeah, yeah! Look, Callie, I'm sorry, but I've got my own problems. Besides, I don't think I'm exactly the person your sister wants to see right now."

"This isn't about you," Callie said coldly.

"Look, I'll call you later," Jake said. "I got major stress."

"Jake, you have to—"

She found herself listening to a dial tone.

She couldn't believe it. Her mind would simply not take it in. He had hung up on her.

This was no time to think about it. Callie flew downstairs, grabbed her purse, and ran out the front door. Her bike had a flat, and the hospital was at least ten miles from her house. She didn't have enough money for a cab, or even a bank card to get more money. Her parents had left all their cash with Laurel for the week.

The idea of asking a neighbor, or running the few

blocks to Leesa or Alexis's house and asking them, or any other number of options, never entered her head. Only this.

Callie sprinted down the street. She turned left at the corner, headed down Magnolia Drive, made a right at the cul-de-sac, and cut through the big park to the street that bordered the other side. Sucking wind the whole two miles, she ran up to Addison's front door, which she pounded on with all her might.

He came to the door and peered at her through the screen. He was wearing #2.

Callie was panting. "Laurel—in the hospital," she managed to gasp.

He opened the screen door, and she tripped into the hallway. "What happened?"

"Car accident," Callie said, still trying to catch her breath. "Hospital called. Look, I know you hate my guts and I know I don't have the right to ask you, but I need money for a taxi to the hospital. I'll pay you back, but please—"

He was already walking away.

"Addison, please!"

"I'm going to call us a taxi," he said over his shoulder.

"Us?" Callie echoed.

"Us," he repeated, pushing up his glasses. "No way I'm letting you go there alone."

"Miss Bailey?"

"Yes?" Callie rushed over to the young nurse. She

and Addison had been pacing the second-floor waiting room for almost two hours.

"You can see your sister now," the nurse said. "Second room on the right."

"Thank you." Callie looked over at Addison.

"Let's go," he said.

They knocked on the door, then pushed it open. Laurel lay there, her face almost as white as the sheets. Her right leg in traction above the bed, encased in a cast from ankle to thigh. Two mean-looking pins stuck out of the cast.

Other than that, and a small bandage on her chin, Laurel looked okay. Pale, though. Addison hung back by the door.

Callie took a few steps toward Laurel's bed. "Laurel?" She could barely get her sister's name out.

Laurel mustered up a weak smile. "Thank God for airbags, huh?"

Callie couldn't help it. She started crying. Then she ran to her sister and hugged her. "Oh, my gosh, am I hurting you?" she cried, pulling away.

"I'm full of painkillers," Laurel said. She put her arms around Callie and weakly hugged her back.

"I'm sorry," Callie sobbed, "I'm so sorry."

"Don't you know never to cry unless you're wearing waterproof mascara?" Laura asked. "You're getting black gunk all over this gorgeous hospital gown."

Callie laughed through her tears and sat up, looking around for a tissue. Addison got the box from the nightstand and handed it to her. Callie wiped her eyes and blew her nose. She looked up at Laurel's tractioned leg.

"What happened?" she asked.

"After I left you and Jake at the agency, I decided to go for a drive around Lake Pontchartrain. I was so furious and so hurt, and—well, I just started driving faster and faster with the music cranked up really loud. It was stupid."

"It's my fault!" Callie bawled.

Laurel shook her head no. "You weren't driving. What I did was stupid. I'm lucky I didn't hurt anyone else and that I got away with just my leg broken in two places. Where's Jake?"

"Band practice," Callie said. "He wouldn't come."

"Figures," Laurel said. "His ego is the biggest thing about him."

"Yeah, I'm beginning to see that," Callie agreed. "It's just that I was in love with him for so long." She shot a look over her shoulder at Addison, but his face was unreadable. "I'm sorry, but it's true," she added softly.

"You love a guy who's so self-centered he wouldn't even bring you to the hospital?" Addison asked, his voice sharp.

Callie bit her lip. "I guess . . . I guess I love—*loved*—who I thought he was."

Laurel's face darkened as she recalled the scene at Bleu Bayou. "Don't mention his name again, or I'll kick you out of this room," Laurel warned. "You and I need to have a very serious talk, Callie. Real soon."

Callie swallowed hard.

"But apparently Jake Moore is less than meets the eye," Laurel giggled. "Wow, that is so funny." She giggled again.

"Pain pills," Addison commented.

"Next time I should slap you twice instead of wrecking my car and my leg," Laurel said and sighed.

The door opened, and the nurse stuck her head into the room. "The doctor wants Laurel to rest," she said. "You two can come back in a couple of hours."

Callie nodded and got up. "You want me to call your friends and tell them you're here?" she asked her sister.

"No" was all Laurel could mumble. "Sleepy."

"Okay, then. Mom and Dad should be at their hotel by now. I'll call and tell them what happened."

"Don't let them freak out and come home," Laurel said softly, her eyes closing. "Dad is supposed to get a big award up there. And they'll kill me for totaling my . . ."

She was snoring before Callie and Addison even got out of the room.

"What do you want to do now?" Addison asked.

"Call my parents." She fished the number out of her purse. "Then get some coffee. I'm not leaving. You go if you want."

"If you're staying, I'm staying," Addison said.

They found a bank of pay phones off the waiting room. Addison called his parents while Callie tried her parents' hotel in Chicago. She got the voice mail of their room and left a message saying that Laurel had been in a car accident, had a broken leg, but was okay and didn't want them to cut their trip short.

Knowing her parents, they'd be on the next plane home anyway.

Callie and Addison took the elevator down to the cafeteria, got two cups of coffee, and sat at an empty table.

"So," Addison began, "what was Laurel talking about some agency?"

Callie sighed and wrapped her hands around her coffee cup. "Modeling agency. I stole some of Laurel's modeling jobs," she confessed. "Her agency wants to sign me. Laurel showed up there when Jake and I were—"

"Spare me the details," Addison interrupted. "My overly vivid imagination can more than fill in the rest." He took a sip of his coffee.

"So, proud of yourself?" he asked.

"No." Callie's voice was so low she barely heard it herself. She stared into the black depths of her coffee.

"I'm sitting here looking at you," Addison said, "and I'm thinking, who is this girl? She doesn't look like the girl I used to know, and she sure doesn't act like the girl I used to know. So. Callie Bailey, who are you?"

Callie gulped hard. "A total moron suffering from temporary insanity?" she ventured.

"That's a start," Addison told her. "And?"

"And . . . I apologize," Callie added.

"And?" Addison prompted again.

"And *what?* I just apologized."

"Yeah." Addison took another sip of his coffee. "So, lemme ask you, Cal. Just out of curiosity. Do you have any idea how pathetic you've become?"

"I—I . . ." she stammered.

"So, now you look like the beautiful people," Addison sneered. "Congrats." He put his hands together and began to applaud.

"Cut it out—"

"Look at you, Callie. You've got it down. Pepto-pink perfect. Plastic girl from a plastic mold with a plastic personality. You're one of the people you used to despise. Hey, I'd call that something to be proud of, wouldn't you?"

"You don't understand, Addison—"

"That's right. I don't. I don't know where my friend Callie is, but I miss her. Whether she loved me back or not, I miss her. She was great. Really great. In every way that counts. Some other girl who's cookie-cutter pretty has taken her place. But I have to tell you, Callie, I don't love that girl—I don't even like her."

Addison's cold gaze held Callie's. She thought about all the terrible things she'd done lately, and a huge lump came to her throat. Her eyes filled with tears, and she was so ashamed she had to look away.

"I don't like her, either, Addison," Callie admitted. "Right now, I wish she'd never been born."

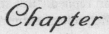

Chapter

10

Callie stepped out of the taxi in front of her house and glanced back at Addison.

"Thank you," she said.

He didn't say a word; he wouldn't even look at her. The taxi took off to take Addison home as Callie walked up the front walkway to the door, reaching in her pocketbook for her front door key.

Down the street the black sedan was parked with its lights off. The man in it watched Callie's arrival with interest through night-vision binoculars.

"That's Subject One, all right, Dr. Warner," the man said to the female driver peering at Callie.

The woman sighed. "I never thought we'd be field-testing Substance Z so soon."

"It didn't happen on purpose—" the man reminded her as Callie put her key in the lock.

"And it's not as if we're controlling her, I know, I know," the woman replied. "But still, it's not as if she volunteered for the project, either."

"I wouldn't parade that point of view around the lab if I were you," the man said. "Uh, she just went inside."

"Then let's go back," the woman told him, and the sedan sped off into the night. "We've got what we came for. Let's put the transmitter on it, and then put it back."

Once she was inside her house, Callie's movements were purposeful. All the way home from the hospital, Callie could think only of what she was going to do when she got home.

She knew exactly what she had to do.

First she went into her bathroom, stripped, and took the longest, hottest, soapiest shower in the history of long, hot, soapy showers. She scrubbed off every trace of her makeup. When she got out of the shower, she didn't bother with the hair dryer, or try to comb out her natural waves. She just put her hair up in a very messy wet ponytail.

She dried off and put on her oldest pair of baggy black pants, a long-sleeved black T-shirt, and unearthed her old black thick-rimmed geeky glasses from her top desk drawer.

Then she went to her closet, methodically took every single article of clothing she had purchased since her makeover day at Threads, and stuffed it all into a huge plastic bag. She dragged the bag into Laurel's room and put it on her bed with a makeshift note on top of it.

"A Gift from Me," the note said. It was the least Callie felt she could do, after wearing so many of Laurel's outfits.

Then Callie went back into the bathroom, swept all her new makeup and hair products into another bag, and put that bag in Laurel's bathroom.

It still wasn't enough. Even doing all these things didn't feel to Callie as if she'd purged the person she had become. So she went back into Laurel's room and dug around in the bag of clothing for the slip dress she had worn to Leesa's party. She took the dress into the backyard, crammed it into the metal grill her family used for cookouts, sprayed it with lighter fluid, and lit a match.

Whoosh! She stared at the flaming dress as its fibers melted. If only she could melt who she had become as easily as she could melt that dress. But scrubbing away her makeup and giving away her clothes couldn't undo all the horrible things she'd done.

Those things she was going to have to live with forever. Forever.

That's when the tears came.

"I'm sorry I ever got gorgeous," she sobbed aloud. "I'm sorry I ever changed because I hate who I am now. I'd do anything just to make myself over into who I used to be, the way I made myself over into what I am now."

Reverse it. Reverse the mirror image.

She blinked, her face eerily illuminated by the

dancing flames. A voice in her head had just spoken to her. And it wasn't her own voice.

"What?" Callie whispered hoarsely.

Reverse it. Reverse the mirror image.

"How?" Callie cried.

You know.

Callie shivered. It was like the voice that had told her to wear clothes that weren't black that day so long ago. It came from the feeling that had led her to the Loverock in the—

The Loverock.

This all started the night of the meteor, she realized. *I found the meteorite, put the Loverock under my pillow, and the next day everything started to change.*

Callie stared into the dying flames. But what she saw was the smoky ring curling up from the ground as she reached into the shallow crater and pulled out the perfect, valentine-shaped diamondlike meteorite.

Suddenly she knew.

"Reverse it. Reverse the mirror image," she whispered. "Sleep with the Loverock under my pillow. Wish to undo what was done."

Callie went back inside, climbed the stairs, and walked into her bedroom.

Something sprang at her with a strangled cry. She screamed, madly reaching for the light switch.

It was the cat, Jumby.

"You scared the heck out of me," Callie said, when she'd composed herself and was sitting on her bed stroking Jumby's fur. "Silly cat."

Her thoughts felt crystal clear now, as if some

strange cloud had lifted. "How's this for weird, Jumby? I actually thought I heard a voice in my head telling me to sleep with the Loverock under my pillow to undo——"

Callie gasped. Because she was looking at the place on her nightstand where she always kept the Loverock.

It was gone.

She put the cat down and lifted the glass dish.

"That's impossible," she muttered. "I never moved it."

Melissa, then? Melissa was the college student from Tulane who cleaned the Baileys' house every Thursday after classes. But Melissa was completely trustworthy. She had been working for the Baileys for two years and had never moved any of Callie's stuff.

Callie started to search her room. By the time she was done, every drawer had been opened, every item of clothing pulled out, and every piece of furniture moved, including the rug.

No Loverock.

Frantic now, she searched the other rooms of the house and left chaos in her wake.

Nothing.

When there was no place else she could search, Callie trudged back up to her room, undressed, and collapsed onto her bed.

"I'm losing it," she muttered. "I just tore this entire house apart looking for a stupid meteorite. Like I really believe that if I slept with it under my pillow I could get my old self back."

You do believe it.

Callie put her hands over her ears. "No, I don't. And why would any sane person want to be a geek instead of beautiful, anyway? Answer? She wouldn't."

She closed her eyes and curled up, beyond exhausted. "Fine," she mumbled, burrowing her head into her pillow. "My Loverock grew legs and walked out of my house."

All that's mumbo jumbo, anyway. If I got obnoxious on my own, I can get un-obnoxious on my own. I don't need some meteorite for that.

An instant later she was fast asleep.

Something woke her up.

Callie sat bolt upright in bed, every nerve end in her body tingling.

Just like that night on the bayou, Callie thought. *It feels exactly the same.*

She had been having the strangest dream. Someone very old, someone she knew, was trying to tell her something very important. But already it was slipping away.

She looked at the luminous hands of the clock on her nightstand. After midnight. She sat a moment, waiting for . . . *something.*

Nothing happened. No voices.

"You have one vivid imagination, Bailey," she muttered. But she was wide awake, and knew it would be pointless to try to go back to sleep. She glanced at her desk and saw her computer.

No time like the present, she told herself. *Get to it. You have a deadline.*

Callie switched on a lamp and got out of bed. She put on a stretched-out set of sweats and walked over to her computer, where she booted up her word processing program and went to work.

GEEKS SPEAK #10

Hey, gang, remember me? So, ask me how it feels to be a walking cliché, poster girl for a tired transformation tale. First there was *Pygmalion*. Which gave birth to *My Fair Lady*. Which brought us *Pretty Woman*. Which spawned *Clueless*. Which morphed into *She's All That*.

And then there's me, Callie Bailey. Geek Girl enters transporter room and emerges as Cute Girl, her life magically changed forever. She gets cool and popular overnight. Hot Guy who formerly never gave Geek Girl the time of day suddenly falls madly in love with Cute Girl.

This is not appearing now at your friendly neighborhood cineplex, either. This is real life. This is my life.

Except for one little wrinkle. That happily-ever-after, fade-to-black thing? I don't think so. I got treated to the ugly side of the Pepto Pinks when one of them tried to kick my friend out of her party because he wasn't cool enough for her.

And then there was Hot Guy Prince Charming. Turns out he isn't very charming after all.

Because the only one he's madly in love with is himself.

How about this for a movie moment? One of the Pepto Pinks, poised to accept the crown as president of The Saints next year, decides it's all a pathetic, shallow, meaningless waste of time. She scrubs off her makeup right there on stage, cuts up her so-called cool clothes, and while she's at it, ditches her so-called cool friends and proudly rejoins the ranks of the unique. Oh, yeah. She also ditches Hot Guy Prince Not-so-Charming and falls for Geek Guy, who was smarter, kinder, funnier, cooler and all around more gorgeous than you-know-who all along.

Now *that's* what I call a happy ending.

Callie nibbled on her thumbnail and reread what she'd just written.

Not bad for a first draft. But before I can really finish it, there's something else I need to do.

She craned her neck to see the clock on her nightstand. Almost two in the morning. She knew she shouldn't do what she was about to do. She knew it was crazy.

But she didn't care.

She pulled on more clothes, a black jean jacket, and hurried downstairs. Jumby rubbed against her leg, happy for company. But she hadn't come downstairs to entertain the cat. She grabbed the house keys. At the moment she was extremely glad that her parents were on vacation and that Laurel wasn't home—because they all would have stopped her from doing what she was about to do.

She went into the garage, got out her tools, and patched the hole in her flat tire. Then she pedaled off into the pitch-black night.

Callie walked her bike up the massive driveway, which was illuminated by pin spots of white lights recessed into the small bushes. The house was huge, with a wide front porch and imposing white columns. When she was close to it, she leaned the bike against one of the columns. Then she gathered up some pebbles and stood under Jake's window.

She threw one. Direct hit.

Tap!

Another toss.

Tap!

And another, with a slightly larger pebble.

A light went on in Jake's room.

"What light through yonder window breaks," she muttered with satisfaction. The window shade was lifted, the window opened, and a sleepy-looking Jake peered out.

"Gee, did I wake you?" Callie called up to him.

"Callie? Are you nuts? It's the middle of the night!"

"No kidding," Callie agreed.

"What are you doing here?" Jake asked.

"In the category of stupid questions of the year, that just got nominated." She threw another pebble, which grazed his arm.

"Ow!"

"Stung, huh?" Callie asked lightly. "Frankly, I never knew I was such a good shot."

"Man, you've lost it. Hold on, I'm coming down."

"What a good idea," Callie mumbled to herself. "So glad it dawned on you."

Thirty seconds later the front door was opened. Jake came out, bare-chested, wearing nothing but a pair of cotton pajama bottoms. He looked perfect. Callie didn't care.

"What is up with you?" he whispered harshly.

"Oh, not much, what's up with you?" she asked cheerfully.

"Jake?" An older woman peered out the window next to Jake's room.

"Sorry, Mom," Jake called up to her. "Go back to sleep."

"What are you doing down there? I was ready to call the police."

"Everything's fine, Mom. Just a friend of mine."

"Oh, for heaven's sake," she muttered, slamming the window shut.

"Nice, Callie," Jake snapped. "Thanks for waking my mother—"

"And thanks for being there when I needed you to take me to the hospital," Callie replied.

"You came here at two-thirty in the morning because you're *ticked off*?" He was incredulous.

She shrugged. "Call it a whim."

"What I call it is—forget it. I'm going back to bed." He started to turn away.

"So soon? You didn't even say anything about how great I look," Callie said. "You like?"

She spun in a circle. And for the first time he noticed her all-black, no-makeup, messy-hair look.

"No, I don't like."

"You know, come to think of it, I don't, either. Oh, I like the clothes," she corrected herself quickly. "It's you I don't like."

Jake shook his head. "Unreal. Just because I'm not at your beck and call—"

"That's really how you see it, isn't it?" Callie marveled. "Aren't you even going to ask me how Laurel is?"

"How is she?"

"Leg broken in two places. But she could be dead. You didn't even think to ask. Thoughtful, Jake."

Jake ran a hand through his hair. "Cut me some slack here, okay? You just woke me up."

"Yeah," Callie agreed. "I feel real bad about it, too. But somehow I just couldn't wait until morning to tell you that we're through."

Jake laughed derisively. "Get real, Callie. No way you're going to break up with me."

"Oh, I'm not *going* to break up with you," Callie said. "Because I already did. I'm clearly not good enough for you, Jake. In fact, the only one who might be is you."

Callie walked over to her bike. "Well, I'm really glad we had this little chat. I feel so much better."

"Oh, you do, do you?" Jake's voice was hard. "You're a loser, Callie. I don't have time for your little games. Believe me, a dozen girls are waiting to take your place."

Callie got on her bike. "The sad thing is, that's probably true. Just one last thing, Jake. Make sure one of them isn't my sister."

"What is that, a threat?"

Callie thought a minute. "Well, in the movies I suppose I'd say, 'No, it's a promise.' Sounds good. But the truth is, yeah. It's a threat."

"Right, geek," Jake taunted her. "I'm real scared."

"You should be," Callie said. Her eyes locked with his. "I have powers you never even dreamed of, Jake."

I have powers you never even dreamed of? Right. Where did that line come from?

But something in the way she had said it stopped him cold.

Jake Moore, Mr. Everything, stood there in the night, speechless, as Callie hopped on her bike and pedaled down his driveway, never looking back.

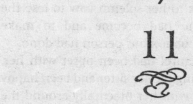

Chapter

11

Callie paced outside the door to her sister's room, reluctant to knock. The past week had been terrible. Laurel started to get mad at her almost as soon as the doctors had taken her off her painkillers. And she'd stayed mad at her. As for her parents, they'd cut short their trip and come straight to the hospital from the airport, to find one daughter in traction and the other daughter responsible for it.

Callie had blurted out everything to them—how she'd sneaked around with Jake, taken Laurel's wardrobe, and stolen Laurel's modeling jobs. She'd hoped it would help lift the terrible burden of guilt from her conscience. So far, that little theory hadn't worked at all.

Ouch. It had been hard to hear her parents say how "deeply disappointed" they were in her.

That line has to come from the Top-Secret Parent Handbook, Callie thought glumly. *Guaranteed to make you feel the self-worth of a salted slug.*

At least she'd stuck to her solemn vow to lose the obnoxious person she had become and to make amends for what that obnoxious person had done.

So, even though Laurel had been upset with her, she had done everything for her sister and been happy to do it. She'd stayed with her practically around the clock until she was released from the hospital. And when she'd come home, Callie had basically waited on her twenty-four/seven.

Jake hadn't called once, and both sisters were glad.

But the two sisters hadn't really talked. In fact, since Laurel had come home four days earlier, they'd barely spoken at all. Callie knew she should apologize, but it was just so hard to say the words.

And even harder to mean them.

Callie took a deep breath. Laurel would be returning to school the next day, so it was now or never.

Callie knocked softly on her sister's door. "Laurel?"

"What?"

"Can I come in?"

"I suppose."

Callie grimaced. This was not going to be easy. She pushed the door open. Laurel was in bed, reading.

She looked up at Callie. She didn't say a word.

"Hi," Callie said tentatively. She came over to the bed. "That nightgown looks good on you."

"You came in to tell me that?" Laurel asked coldly.

"No. It was an observation."

"Fascinating. I'd jot it down, but I'm too bored. What did you want?"

Callie sat, fingering a button on her shirt, trying to figure out what she wanted to say. "So, how are you feeling?" was what finally came out of her mouth.

"Gee, just great," Laurel said sarcastically. "How charming of you to inquire."

Callie was taken aback. Sarcasm was *her* domain. Laurel was *never* sarcastic. It was weird, coming out of Laurel's mouth. Kind of scary, even.

"Look, I know you're mad—"

"Brilliant deduction," Laurel snapped. "Aren't you the mental giant."

Callie's jaw fell open. "You know who you sound like? You sound like . . . me."

Laurel raised her eyebrows.

"It feels horrible to have someone talk to you that way," Callie realized out loud. She searched her mind for the right word. "Small. That's it. It makes you feel diminished."

"I know," Laurel said softly. She sounded like herself again, not like Callie at all.

And that's when it dawned on Callie. "You're acting like me on purpose, aren't you?"

Laurel nodded. "You're always so busy trying to prove that you're independent and just too brilliant and hip to care about what anyone else thinks. But you never think about how that makes people feel—"

"Well, what about you?" Callie challenged. "You'd sell out your own family if it meant staying in with the too-cool crowd—"

"I would not!"

"No? Then why are you friends with a total witch like Leesa Deerfield? You know she kicked Addison out of her party because he didn't meet her perfect people standards. And if I looked like I used to look, she would have kicked me out, too. And you would have let her."

The silence in the room was deafening as the sisters stared angrily at each other.

"Leesa Deerfield has a lot of power," Laurel finally explained, her voice low.

"Only if you give it to her," Callie said. "God, Laurel, you're nicer to her than you are to me. And she's way down there on the food chain. How do you think that makes me feel?"

"I guess I never thought about it," Laurel admitted.

"Yeah, well, I sure wish you'd think about it now."

"But you don't care what anyone thinks—"

"And you care what *everyone* thinks!" Callie exclaimed. "Oh, wait. Not everyone. Only the cool, beautiful and popular. Which always left out your geeky little sister."

"I care about you," Laurel protested. "I care about you enough not to have said anything when you were going into my room and taking all my clothes without asking. Did you think I didn't notice? Of course I noticed. But I thought: hey, let my little sister shine. She deserves it."

"If you can be friends with people like Leesa who are mean to me, how am I supposed to believe that you care about me?" An ache welled up in the back of Callie's throat, and she willed herself not to cry.

Laurel bit her lower lip. "You want to know the truth? I can't stand Leesa Deerfield."

"Then why are you friends with her?"

"It's hard to explain, Callie. It's like . . . ever since I was little, Mom and Dad and everyone said I was so pretty and sweet and everyone loved me. And I thought . . . I guess I always thought that if I stopped being pretty and sweet all the time, maybe no one would love me."

"But it isn't true!" Callie insisted.

Laurel shrugged sadly. "I don't know if it is or isn't, but I've always *felt* like it's true. And I've always felt so jealous of you, because you were so independent and self-confident, and you say exactly what you really think."

"And I've always felt so jealous of you for being pretty and perfect and popular and everything that I'm not."

They stared at each other, amazed. And then they both burst out laughing.

"I had no idea—" they both began at the same time.

And then they both convulsed into laughter again.

"Callie, I'm so sorry—" Laurel began.

"No, no, please let me say it first," Callie begged. "What I did to you was so terrible, Laurel. When I think about how bad that car accident could have been, and how it's all my fault—"

"Look, no one made me drive like an idiot," Laurel

said. "No matter how upset I was, I have to take re-sponsibility for that. So you can stop beating yourself up, Callie."

"I'm still the one who lied and sneaked around and betrayed you." Callie swallowed around the lump in her throat.

"True," Laurel said. "So I guess you can just slap yourself around a little."

Callie smiled sadly. "I was so jealous of you, all those years, and I used it as an excuse to turn into the kind of person that I hate. And there's no excuse for that. I'm so, so sorry." Now the tears spilled over. Be-cause she hadn't just said the words. At last she had fi-nally meant them.

There were tears in Laurel's eyes, too. "I'm sorry too, Cal. You're right about Leesa. She's right up there on the witch-o-meter." She smiled wistfully. "Hey, maybe if I got some of your good qualities and you got some of my good qualities—"

"It's not that easy," Callie said softly.

Laurel sighed. "I know. The truth is, I don't know if I'll ever stand up to Leesa. Or stop caring about being popular and fitting in. It's just who I am."

"And I don't know if I'll ever stop feeling a certain amount of disdain for people who care so much about being popular and fitting in," Callie said. "But . . ." She thought for a moment. "That doesn't mean we can't . . . broaden our emotional horizons," she added airily.

Laurel laughed, and Callie did, too. Then impetu-ously Callie hugged her sister, and Laurel hugged her back.

"Let's make a deal, Cal," Laurel said. "Sisters come before friends."

"And before *boyfriends*," Callie added firmly.

"*Definitely*," Laurel agreed.

They shook on it, smiling at each other. For the first time in a long, long time, Callie felt proud that she was Laurel Bailey's sister.

The next morning Callie, dressed in her most comfortable black pants, and a pink cotton camisole under a black cotton cardigan, stood just inside the front doors to the school, talking to Addison's mom on the pay phone.

"Addison and his dad have tickets to see *Rent* at the Wood Theater downtown," Ms. Pate said, "so there's no chance that he'll be here."

"Great," Callie said. "You're really sure it's okay?"

"Callie, it's fine. Come anytime after seven-thirty tomorrow night."

"Okay. Thanks again." Callie hung up and walked over to Laurel, who was leaning on her crutches, surrounded by an adoring public waiting to sign her cast. A slender sky blue ribbon was wrapped around it, color-coordinated with Laurel's sky blue skirt.

"Are you okay?" Callie asked her. "There's a chair right there, you know."

"I'm fine," Laurel assured her. "Happy to be back."

Callie laughed. "That's something you will never hear me say in this lifetime."

"Oooh, I'm signing, too," one of the cheerleaders said, pulling the top off a neon pink marker.

"You can go if you want, Callie," her sister said.

"No prob, Laurel, I can carry you to your classes," a cute guy from the football team offered.

"I'm waiting for you," Callie insisted. "I want to make sure you're all right."

Callie leaned against the wall, watching as everyone signed her sister's cast. As she watched, the cute guy from the football team proved how easily he could lift Laurel and her cast.

Callie had figured her parents would lay some massive punishment on her—ground her for life, maybe. But they hadn't. Interesting. They said they had a feeling she had already punished herself enough. They hadn't allowed her to sign with Bleu Bayou Model and Talent, however. She could freelance the same way Laurel freelanced. Period.

In some strange way, Callie was glad.

As for Addison and Sarah and the rest of her geek friends, Callie was doing her best to repair the damage she had done. It wasn't easy. But when her "Geeks Speak" article had come out a few days ago, it had helped. Sarah had come up to her, told her how great it was, and asked Callie if she wanted to go see a Truffaut film at the French Film Festival that weekend.

But things with Addison were still pretty awful. He spoke to her, but never about anything. It felt as if they were strangers. Callie knew she'd hurt him badly. And she didn't know if she could ever get him to trust her again.

But she was sure going to try.

"You ready to get to class?" Callie asked her sister.

"I really can handle it, Callie. Besides, the crutches are guaranteed to give me the sympathy vote."

"You're not running for anything, as I recall," Callie reminded her.

"Well, prom queen, but not for a few months," Laurel said, shrugging. "By then the cast will be off. Too bad."

Callie laughed. Laurel would never change. Which was not necessarily such a bad thing.

"So, in the words of Will, 'Lay on, Macduff,'" Callie said, cocking her head at her sister.

"Can I help?" Jonny Alvarez asked. About the same height as Laurel, cute in a Freddy Prinze Jr. kind of way, he was one of the guys in the senior class whom Callie actually respected. Bound for Rice in the fall, he played varsity soccer and was in the Reading Is Fundamental volunteer program in the local elementary schools.

"Laurel?" Callie asked.

"Fine with me, thanks." Laurel gave Jonny a heart-melting smile, and Callie handed him Laurel's books. She leaned over and whispered in Laurel's ear, "Big sister, things are definitely looking up."

Callie watched as Laurel made her way down the hall on her crutches, Jonny beside her.

She's more graceful on crutches than most people are dancing, Callie thought. *And I think instead of resenting it, I'm proud of her. Huh.*

"Hey," a voice said behind her.

She turned around. Addison.

Outfit #1.

"Hi. How's it going?"

He shrugged. "More fun and adventure at the amusement park of high school. Do your trig?"

"Yeah. But I didn't understand half of it."

He shrugged again. "You could have called me."

"Yeah, but . . ." Everything was so weird between them. All the ease she'd taken for granted had turned into an invisible wall that separated them. How did you tear down a wall you couldn't even see?

One invisible brick at a time, Callie thought.

She took a deep breath. "So, listen. I kinda . . . have something for you."

"Oh?"

"Yeah," she said. "An invitation."

"To what?"

"It's a surprise."

"I see." Addison pushed his glasses up his nose. "Dare I ask what kind of surprise?"

"You dare, but I'm not telling," Callie said.

"Am I putting my life in danger?"

"Highly doubtful," Callie said.

"And just when does this surprise take place?"

"Just be by your telephone on Sunday afternoon, at around one, and the rest, as they say, will come clear."

"Today is Tuesday," Addison pointed out. "I'm being invited to sit by my phone on Sunday? To hear about something that you're not telling what it is?"

"I marvel at your ability to grasp the details," Callie said, walking backward away from him. "See ya in homeroom."

She hurried around the corner toward her locker. Alexis Monroe and Jim Kagen were heading in the other direction. They whispered to each other—obviously about her—then laughed derisively.

Callie blew them a kiss and kept walking. What they thought of her or whispered about her mattered even less than Jake Moore mattered. As for Jake, she had seen him the day before, in the parking lot, in his Jeep, some cute platinum-blond transfer student cuddling up next to him. For just a moment that old feeling had come over her again—longing for the boy she could never get.

Then she'd remembered: had him, dumped him, glad about it.

And she'd laughed.

In fact, as she spun the combination on her locker, she laughed again, just thinking about it.

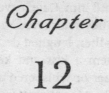
"*H*i!" a young woman on a ladder changing a light-bulb called down to Callie as Callie ran breathlessly into the studio. "You're the model, right?"

"Yeah, I'm Callie Bailey, and I'm so sorry I'm late, really."

"No prob, Eric's running late, too. I'm Jana Kendall, the P.A.—you know, production assistant—better known as slave." She climbed down the ladder and shook Callie's hand. "Welcome."

"Thanks," Callie said, swiping some loose hair off her face. "I was planning to borrow my sister's car after school, but it wouldn't start, so I had to take two buses, and then I got off at the wrong stop and walked the wrong way, and—"

"Hey, breathe!" Jana laughed. "If you'd been on time, you'd be the first punctual model I've met this month. Besides, Eric really *is* running way behind. He had to redo a few catalog shots this morning, and he went way overtime, perfectionist that he is. Have you ever worked with him before?"

Callie shook her head no.

"Well, you're gonna have a blast. Eric Rink is a great guy, plus he's funny, plus he's the best there is. Which is why I stick around for slave wages. Have a seat, he'll be right out. I know he'll want to meet with you before you get into makeup and wardrobe."

Callie plopped down in one of the old red velvet theater chairs that lined the waiting area of the studio and sighed with relief.

It was the next day. She'd been restless the night before, tossing and turning, finally falling asleep around two. Then she'd overslept, waking up as foggy as if she'd been drugged. She'd barely had time to throw on her clothes and run out the door to drive herself and Laurel to school.

She hadn't even had a chance to look at herself in the mirror.

Then her trig teacher had sprung a pop quiz on them. And her sadistic phys-ed teacher decided it was the perfect day for running wind sprints.

At the end of the day Jonny was giving Laurel a ride home so that Callie could take Laurel's car to her modeling job, but the car wouldn't start. She freaked—she barely had enough time to get to the gig as it was. Fortunately, Jonny offered to come back and take care of it.

What a nice guy. And he certainly seemed to like Laurel.

Callie leaned her head back against the wall. She felt grubby, exhausted, and as un–model-like as it was humanly possible to feel.

She pulled her job slip out of her bag. The client had booked her on the basis of other shots of her he'd seen, without a go-see, so she'd never met the photographer. It was a print shoot for a national chain of stores called Finyl Vinyl. They specialized in out-of-print albums and vintage tapes, and also sold new CDs.

Callie picked up an old issue of *Spin* and flipped through it. Now that she was a model, she had begun to pay attention to the photo credits in magazines. A photo of Jewel in that issue of *Spin*, sprawled and laughing in a field of daisies, was credited to Eric Rink.

Impressive.

"So, Callie, found my photo in there yet?" a warm masculine voice asked.

Callie looked up.

Eric Rink.

His smile lit up his handsome face. He was tall—six feet, maybe—with short auburn hair and a silver quarter-moon stud in one ear. He wore a black T-shirt under a black silk blazer, black jeans, and black work boots.

The definitive geek chic outfit, Callie couldn't help thinking as she studied him. But what really stunned Callie was how young he looked. Really, really young.

Like, no more than eighteen.

"The answer to your burning question is, seventeen," Eric said. "I can read your mind." He held out his hand.

Callie shook it. "I didn't mean to—" she began.

He laughed. "Hey, it's okay. Everyone gets that same look on their face when they first meet me. I'm used to it."

"Were you a child prodigy or something?"

He laughed again. "More like the son of an extremely famous mother. Does the name Gloria McSweeney ring any bells?"

"Are you kidding?" Callie asked. "She did that photo book last year of all the rock stars—it's fantastic. And she's the host of *House of Glory.*" Callie named a famous fashion television show on one of the cable music channels. "She's your—"

"Mom? Yep," Eric filled in. "She likes to think photography is in my bloodline. Which is kinder than saying it's just pure nepotism, don't you think?"

Now Callie laughed. "If you weren't good, it probably wouldn't matter who your mom was, though. Do you live in New Orleans?"

"Mom's guest artist-in-residence at Tulane for the semester, so I came along for the ride."

"So you already finished high school, then," Callie guessed, disappointed. After all, what if it turned out he was a senior and he was about to transfer into St. Charles Parish Regional High School, and—

Watch it, Callie, she cautioned herself. *Your dreams have gotten you into a heap of trouble already, remember?*

"Well, there's another weird thing about me," Eric said. "I never went to high school. I was home-schooled by my dad. Got my GED when I was sixteen."

"Wow. Is your dad a photographer, too?" Callie asked.

Eric's face clouded. "He was a painter, but he died last year."

Callie gulped. "I'm really sorry—"

"It's okay." Eric managed a smile. "I still talk to him all the time. Told you I was weird. So, you ready to get into makeup? Jana's around here somewhere—"

"At your beck and call, maestro," Jana teased as she hurried down the hall.

"She's all yours," Eric told her. "Can we get her on the set in—"

"Thirty," Jana filled in. "Because you're running behind. What a shocker." Jana crooked her finger at Callie. "Come with me. Fortunately, I'm a cosmetics genius."

Jana took Callie into the hair-and-makeup room. There was no mirror, but Callie knew better than to try to give any input to the makeup artist, anyway. She was a hired face. What they wanted, they got.

Jana chatted away as she did Callie's face, then she brought in the outfit they wanted her in just as Eric peeked in. "Hey, don't have her change clothes," he said.

"Run that by me again," Jana suggested.

"I kinda love what you've got on, Callie," he explained. "If you don't mind . . ."

Callie looked down at her baggy black overalls, worn over a tiny stretch red and black T-shirt. "This?"

"Sure. It's casual, fun, unique. Suits you," Eric said.

Callie shrugged. "Fine with me."

"Hair?" Jana asked.

Eric cocked his head to the side and studied Callie's messy ponytail. "I like it. Some little barrettes and things, that's all."

"Your quirky wish is my command," Jana said. She scrunched some gel into the ends of Callie's hair, then put in some glittery barrettes. "There you go." Jana removed the tissues she'd tucked into Callie's neckline to keep the makeup off her. "You're a goddess. I ran over, so hustle yourself into the studio, please."

A representative from Finyl Vinyl was putting the last touches on the set for the shoot. The backdrop was made of oversize record albums surrounding a huge old-fashioned–looking banner of a cheerleader, holding a megaphone for Finyl Vinyl.

"Sit, Callie, please," Eric told her, pointing to the overstuffed chair on the set.

Callie sat.

"No, no, not like that," Eric said to her through his viewfinder. "Like you're home alone, totally relaxed, in your most comfortable chair."

Impulsively Callie threw her legs over one side of the chair and flung her head back.

"I love that!" Eric exclaimed, clicking off a few shots. "I have to tell you, Callie, you look very different from the photos that Geneva sent over."

"I do?"

"Yeah. At first I wasn't sure, but . . . I think this is gonna work. Your look is much fresher, more original, more beautiful than pretty. Less cookie-cutter."

Callie grinned and Eric clicked off a few quick shots.

"Hey, she's original, just like Finyl Vinyl," the middle-aged, ponytailed store rep cheered. "I like that. Hey, Callie, what's your favorite oldies group?"

"Blondie, of course," Callie replied.

"An original with taste," the rep said. He popped the *Parallel Lines* tape into the sound system, and music filled the studio.

"All right, Callie Bailey, original," Eric said, "let's get to work."

Time flew by. Callie felt really comfortable with Eric behind the camera. He had her jump up and down on the chair as if she were having a tantrum, had her swing her legs over the chair back and lean her head upside down toward the floor, just like a little kid. She blew bubbles with bubble gum, fanned herself with a giant paper fan, hit a yoga pose, whatever came into either her head or Eric's.

"I think that's a wrap, girl," Eric finally said. "Great work."

"That rocked!" the store rep cried happily, giving Callie a big thumbs-up as Jana tossed Callie and Eric cold bottles of mineral water. "Finyl Vinyl—original. Yeah!"

"Thanks," Callie said, and guzzled hers gratefully. She held the sweating bottle to her forehead. "Whew. I'm roasting."

"Boy, I'd love to make some cheesy comment right now about how hot you are," Eric said. "But I just don't think I can pull it off."

"I don't, either," Callie said, laughing.

"Even though, of course, it's true." His eyes met hers. Big, brown flecked with gold. Intelligent and honest.

"You're flirting with me," Callie observed.

"A distinct possibility," Eric agreed.

Callie shook her head ruefully. "Life is so funny. Because you wouldn't have given me the time of day six months ago."

"Why, did the wicked witch cast a spell on you?" Eric teased.

"Something like that."

"Well, for what it's worth, I am not Joe Photographer Stud. I never flirt with models."

"Never?" Callie echoed.

"Hardly ever," Eric amended with a grin. "Seriously. I'd like the opportunity to get to know you better. Wow, that sounded formal, huh?"

Callie threw her head back and laughed, and a rhinestone barrette in her hair glinted light into an old-fashioned wooden-framed mirror near the wall. Callie hadn't even realized it was there.

Now she turned to it, as did Eric. He smiled at her into the mirror, raising his water bottle in salute.

"Callie Bailey, can I take you out for coffee?"

Callie barely heard him.

Because the girl staring back at her in the mirror was her old self. With great makeup. And a sparkle in her eyes, and a self-confident flush to her cheeks.

But still, her old self.

"So, can I take your silence as a yes?" Eric asked.

Callie was speechless.

"Listen, I really don't make a habit of going out with models," he said earnestly. "So I'm probably not doing this very well, but—"

"I . . . I have to go," Callie said, backing away from the mirror.

"Hey, are you okay?" Eric asked. "You look like you just saw a ghost."

Callie never answered. She grabbed her stuff, fled, and called a taxi from the lobby. She never thanked Jana or thanked the rep from Finyl Vinyl or said good-bye to Eric.

Eric was right. She *had* seen a ghost.

And she was it.

Callie slammed the door to the taxi and ran up to the house.

Down the street the black sedan was parked safely out of view.

"You're sure you've got it back in her room?" the woman behind the wheel asked her crew-cut companion.

The man nodded. "No one was home. She'll find it soon enough."

"And the radio transmitter is functioning?"

"I put it in myself," the man said. "She'll never find it. But we'll be able to track the Substance Z sample wherever she takes it."

"I hope so," the woman said. "I hope so." Her eyes went back to the front door, and she watched Callie let herself inside.

"Callie honey?" her dad called from the bedroom as

Callie let herself in. "Is that you? We just got home ourselves."

"Yeah, Dad. I'm fine. I'm going to bed." She bounced up the stairs, went into her room and closed her door, and put her back against it.

"Okay, calm down," she told herself aloud. "You are not losing your mind. It was a . . . a fluke of light. Right."

I'll just sit down for a minute and calm down, she decided. *Then I'll get up and look at myself in the mirror, and I'll look like I looked yesterday. Fine. What a sensible plan.*

She slowly sat on her bed. Something sharp poked into her butt.

"Ouch!" She got up and looked under her quilt. Nothing. She lifted the covers up. Nothing. She lifted the mattress up.

There was the Loverock.

But I couldn't possibly have felt it by sitting on the bed, Callie thought. *Only I did.*

All the little hairs on the back of her neck stood up.

"Okay, I only feel like I'm losing my mind," she said out loud. "The Loverock was under my mattress. That means I slept on it. Which is what I thought I needed to do to undo the—"

She could feel the color drain from her face.

The Loverock had been missing. Now it was back. And clearly, if it was under her mattress, she had slept on it.

And Callie Bailey had undone her dream.

Chapter

13

🎵

*S*unday morning Callie sat cross-legged on her bed, talking with Eric Rink on the phone. It had taken days and all her nerve for her to call him and apologize. But all she'd gotten was his answering service, so she'd left a message asking him to call her.

That had been on Friday. She hadn't heard from him until just now. She'd already decided that he thought she was some kind of total flake and didn't ever plan to return her call. But he explained that he'd been out of town on a shoot and had just gotten back late the night before.

The funny thing was, he thought it was he who'd blown his chances with her, by hitting on her at the end of the Finyl Vinyl shoot.

Now, *that* was hilarious.

"So, listen, Callie," Eric said. "A songwriter friend of

mine is performing at Hava Java coffeehouse in Overton on Wednesday night. Am I risking a hang-up if I invite you?"

Callie laughed. "Your ear is safe. I'd love to go."

"Great, that's great. I'll pick you up at eight, okay?"

"Fine. Let me give you directions. Take the—"

"I confess, I know where you live," Eric said sheepishly.

Callie was surprised but decided to play it cool. "So that was you out there, casing my house for robbery," she joked.

"Actually, that was me thinking I might leave flowers and a note of abject apology on your doorstep," Eric admitted. "And then, basically beg shamelessly for you to call me."

"Gee, if I'd known, I would have held out and not called. I love flowers."

"Well, I'll remember that," Eric said warmly. "I'll see you Wednesday, Callie. I really am glad you called."

"Me, too. Bye." Callie hung up the phone and hugged her knees to her chin. Eric Rink liked her. *Really* liked her, it seemed. And Eric Rink, frankly, left Jake Moore in the dust.

She got up to look at herself in the mirror. Though her body was still lean, because she had kept up her running, she looked exactly as she had before her big transformation.

Exactly the same. And yet completely different, she realized.

She smiled at her reflection. A cute, confident-looking girl smiled back.

She went to her nightstand and picked up the Loverock. The perfect, glittering heart lay in the palm of her hand.

"This was me all the time," Callie said, curling her fingers around the Loverock. "I just never knew it."

"Ah, is the blindfold absolutely necessary?" Addison asked as Callie led him downstairs into her basement.

"For the moment. Just one more step down."

Addison gingerly made the final step. "Now what?"

"Now keep walking," Callie said, leading him slowly by the hand. "You're doing great."

"Gee, thanks. When you told me the big Sunday surprise was that I was supposed to come over to your house, no questions asked, I had no idea you planned to blindfold me at the front door and drag me down here. Which, as I recall, you use even less than we use our basement."

"Remember when you and I decided to enter the science fair together in fifth grade?" Callie asked, leading him along. "It's where we set up a lab."

"And cooked up something that smelled like rotten eggs," Addison recalled, laughing.

"My parents had it fumigated three times and then gave up." Callie pulled him to a stop.

"We've stopped," Addison noted.

"Perceptive. I like that about you."

"Now what?" Addison asked.

"Now shut up," Callie replied sweetly. "I'm savoring the moment."

She had spent all week getting ready. Two days had been spent cleaning out the basement—her parents were still in a state of shock over that one. Then she'd proceeded to transform the basement into a French café.

She'd covered cardboard boxes with various pieces of fabric she'd found in the attic. She'd put candles on all the boxes. The old iron patio table, draped with a floral sheet, was the café's only table. The table was set for two, and a vase of lavender tulips, Addison's favorite flower, was the centerpiece. Next to the table, a champagne bucket full of ice held a sweating bottle of sparkling grape juice.

"Do let me know when you're done savoring whatever it is you're savoring," Addison said.

"Just one sec." Callie hurried to the tape deck and started a cassette. Edith Piaf's legendary voice filled the room.

"And now, *monsieur*," Callie said with her best French accent, as she untied his blindfold, "I welcome you to Café des Geeks. *Et voilà!*"

Addison looked around, his jaw hanging open. "It's rather . . . spectacular." He looked at Callie for the first time—she'd made him close his eyes before she'd even open the front door to her house—and burst out laughing.

She had drawn a curling black handlebar mustache over her upper lip.

"Ze *monsieur* finds zum-zing *amusant?*" Callie asked.

"It's entirely possible that you've lost your mind, Callie Bailey."

"Or found it," Callie said quietly. She pulled out a chair for him. "Your table, *monsieur.*"

Addison sat, and Callie poured him a glass of sparkling grape juice, then she poured herself one. "I propose a toast," she said, lifting her glass.

He lifted his, and waited.

"To my best friend in the world, Addison Pate," Callie said, "who I hope can forgive me for being an idiot even if I don't deserve to be forgiven because his friendship means more to me than anyone else's in the whole world."

"A run-on sentence of dubious structure," Addison said, trying and failing to hide how touched he was.

"Editing aside, are we drinking to it or not?"

The candlelight reflected in his shining eyes. "We're drinking to it." He clinked his glass to hers, and they both sipped their juice.

Callie uncovered the dish on the table with a flourish. "Pâté? Stinky cheese?"

He cut himself a wedge of cheese, put it on his plate, and took a piece of the French bread from the basket. "You didn't have to do this, you know."

Callie fingered her wineglass. "Yeah, I did. I just . . . I guess I kinda lost my mind there for a while. It was like—like I was getting to live out a fantasy. And I didn't think about anyone but myself, you know?"

Addison nodded.

She stared thoughtfully at her juice. "Sarah has this quote up on the bulletin board in her room, some sociologist's. W. I. Thomas, I think his name was. 'A sit-

uation defined as real becomes real in its conse-
quences,' " Callie quoted. "She says it helps with her
acting. But I never really understood what that quote
meant. Until now."

Addison's eyes questioned her.

"It's like, when I saw myself as the sister who could
only live in Laurel's shadow, that's how everyone else
saw me, too," Callie struggled to explain. "But now
that I see myself as someone who's okay and interesting and maybe even pretty in her own right, that's
how everyone sees me—well, *almost* everyone—even
though I look pretty much the same. Does that make
any sense?"

Addison gave her a small, wistful smile. "I always
knew you were beautiful. And infinitely more interesting than your sister."

Callie bit her lower lip. It was true. He had always
thought that. And she had never truly appreciated it—
or how much it meant to her.

"Hey, come over here," Callie said, jumping up, and
cocking her head toward the old love seat in the center of the room. "I was supposed to lead up to the big
finale gradually, but . . ."

She took his hand and led him over to the love
seat. "Sit," she commanded. Then she went to what
looked like another large cardboard box covered by
material, yanked the material away, and unveiled an
old TV set.

"That's the TV we used to watch when we were
kids!" Addison exclaimed. "Amazing. It's a dinosaur."

"Even more amazing is that it still works." Callie

pushed a tape into the VCR she had hooked up to the TV.

"Clarissa?" Addison asked. "We never missed it."

"Something better," Callie said. She sat down next to him, the remote in her hand. She started the tape.

The theme to *Dawson's Creek* filled the air. The video opened with stills of Addison and Callie in nursery school.

"This is the video I made for you!" Addison exclaimed. "Where . . . how?"

"I'm in cahoots with your mom," Callie admitted. "She told me about the tape you made for me, and I kind of . . . liberated it."

"Stole it," Addison corrected, but he didn't sound at all angry. His eyes were glued to the screen, to them dancing at Jenny Sheppard's bat mitzvah. Then the scenes from their various favorite TV shows began, and ended, of course, with Dawson and Joey.

And then Addison was looking at himself, sitting on the swing. Making his big romantic confession.

"And that's Addison and Callie," Addison's taped self said, staring into the camera.

Addison's real self pushed his glasses up his nose, both touched and acutely embarrassed. "Feel free to pretend that the final little soliloquy on the swings never happened," he offered self-consciously.

That should have been the end of the tape, but as Addison watched, Callie now appeared, sitting on the same swing he had been sitting on.

"So, I hope you're not too ticked that I liberated— permanently borrowed—basically *stole* the tape you made," Callie-on-tape said into the camera. "And I also hope you don't mind that I added this postscript. Sarah is helping me—she's holding the camera—hi, Sarah!"

Callie-on-tape waved at the camera, which bounced up and down as if it was waving back.

"What I wanted to say," Callie-on-tape continued, "is that this tape is the nicest present anyone ever gave me. Was *going* to give me, I should say, but I kinda wrecked that. You're right, Addison. We've been best friends forever. And one of us is sure we should be boyfriend and girlfriend and one of us isn't sure.

"Maybe it's because that one has thought of you as my friend for so long. Maybe it's because I'm afraid that if we change our relationship, we'll lose what we have. The thought of that scares me to death, Addison."

Sitting there, next to Addison, Callie could feel tears coming to her eyes again, just as they had at the same point when she'd been making the tape. She watched her taped self laugh nervously and push away a tear.

"So, from your best friend, who maybe someday can be something more," the tape continued, "know this, Addison. You are worth ten thousand Jake Moores. You are all that *and* a bag of chips, and I happen to love you with all my heart."

The tape went blank. Callie clicked it off. Edith Piaf had stopped singing long ago. The basement was very, very quiet. Addison was staring down at the floor.

"You hated it," Callie guessed.

"Yeah, Bailey, it stunk." He cleared his throat and quickly wiped something off his cheek.

That was when Callie realized—Addison was sobbing.

"I'm hoping those are the good kinda tears," Callie ventured.

"Manly men like me don't cry, so it must be a cinder in my eye," Addison said. He took a deep breath, and finally looked at her. "Thanks."

"No, thank *you*," Callie said.

"No, thank *you!*"

"No, thank—"

They both burst out laughing.

Addison reached for her hand. "Someone should do a TV series about us."

"How about us?" Callie suggested. "We're the two best writers I know. Just one thing."

"What's that?"

"Sarah gets to play me," Callie said. "She deserves to finally get a lead."

Addison's cheeks grew red. "Speaking of Sarah, well, I invited her to the school dance next week."

Callie was shocked. "You—"

"What surprises you more, that I asked her out or that I'm voluntarily going to a school dance?" Addison asked.

"Both," Callie admitted. "Did she say yes?"

Addison nodded. "I like her, Cal. She's not you, but—"

"It's okay," Callie said quickly. "I like her, too. And I guess I should tell you I met a guy I like."

Addison shrugged. "So, I guess the stars of the show are, for the moment, dating other people."

"Looks that way," Callie agreed. "But I have no idea who they'll be with by the end of the season."

"Me neither," Addison said. "But I do know that they'll still be best friends. Forever."

"Forever," Callie echoed. She flipped the VCR off and the TV on, and changed stations until she found *The Wonder Years* on cable.

"This is the best episode, when he starts this terrible band called The Electric Shoes, remember?" Addison cried.

"Right, I love this one!"

Addison put his arm around Callie, and she leaned against him, happily watching the TV, home once more.

She didn't know whether the Loverock had magically changed her life, or if she had somehow just changed it herself.

But she knew this much: she had her best friend back.

And she knew it wasn't the end of the story.

Epilogue

"*B*ut why would you give it to me?" Sarah asked Callie, as she caressed the glittering Loverock with her hands.

Callie shrugged. "I just want to."

Sarah looked at her as if she were crazy.

"Okay, how about if I say that the voices in my head told me to give it away?" Callie explained.

Sarah laughed. "Well, if the voices in your head tell you to, like, drive around with your eyes closed or something, be sure to mention it to your nearest and dearest friends before you take action, right?"

"You betcha," Callie agreed.

There's no point in telling her that I'm afraid to keep it around here anymore, Callie thought. *Not when I know what a skeptic she is.*

"Well, thanks," Sarah said. "I really love it."

Suddenly Callie had qualms. What if the Loverock really did have some kind of bizarre powers? Powers that, for a while there, had caused her unbelievable trouble and heartache?

Was she offering it to Sarah because Sarah had a date with Addison, and she wanted to hurt her?

"Listen, I know this sounds crazy, Sarah," Callie said slowly, "but on second thought, I changed my mind. That rock might be—I don't know—bad luck or something."

"Look, if you just want to keep it—"

"It's not that," Callie insisted. "It's just that I think the rock might have—okay, this is going to sound really out there—magic powers."

"I'm an actress, Callie, not an idiot," Sarah said.

"Right, forget it. Just be careful about what you wish for, okay?"

"Fine," Sarah said, laughing. "I'll wish for world peace. And a lead in a high school play before I graduate."

"Cool," Callie said, nodding.

Sarah stuck the Loverock into her backpack and slung it over a shoulder. "Well, I gotta run. I'm baby-sitting tonight for the world's brattiest four-year-old. But his parents tip great." She hesitated. "Listen, Addison told me that he told you that he—"

"Invited you to the school dance," Callie filled in. "I think it's great."

"You do?" Sarah asked. "You're sure?"

147

"Totally," Callie said, hugging her friend. "I've even been thinking about inviting this cool guy I met to the dance. His name is Eric. Well, stay tuned."

"That'd be great." Sarah hugged Callie again, and hurried downstairs to get her bike. She had a four-mile bike ride to her house, and Mr. Paulson was picking her up for her baby-sitting job in an hour.

As she climbed onto her bike, she didn't realize that the small hole in the bottom of her ancient backpack had grown much larger, and that the friction of the Loverock against the fraying material was making the hole larger still.

About a mile into her trip, Sarah whizzed through an intersection and hit a small bump. The bike bounced, and Sarah quickly regained control. But the glittering Loverock burst through the hole in her backpack and clattered to the pavement.

Sarah never noticed a thing. Especially not that the jiggling of the Loverock in her backpack had dislodged its tiny homing transmitter. And that while the Loverock now lay in the road, the transmitter was still in her backpack.

And neither did anyone in the black sedan that was following her. They just followed Sarah all the way home.

The Loverock lay on the road, until the rear wheels of a large truck kicked it up into the flatbed of a pickup truck headed in the other direction.

That woman in the pickup truck found the glittering Loverock when she got home, which was fifteen miles away. That weekend, she gave it to her teen granddaughter, Marilee.

Marilee was in the tenth grade. She was a sweet girl. She worked hard. She loved her family, her friends, and the stray animals that she'd take care of until she could find them good homes. She was an outstanding young photographer, who many people said looked like a brunette version of the singer Jewel.

Marilee and her father didn't have a lot of money, which wasn't important at all when they'd lived in the working-class town of Carter. Now that they were living in wealthy Overton, where her father was the caretaker for a rich family's estate, it was sometimes difficult. Several girls at school would goof on her because she had to buy clothes at Wal-Mart and not at the expensive stores in Overton Square.

Worst of all, Marilee had told her grandmother, was that she couldn't afford to buy a new gown for the winter formal at school.

The grandmother didn't have a lot of money, either. There wasn't much she could give to Marilee, other than love. So she impetuously gave Marilee the glittering, heart-shaped rock she'd found in her pickup.

And the thing about Marilee was this: she had a dream.

She thought about it every night, before she fell asleep. Yes, she wanted a great camera of her own and a darkroom. And a bigger shelter for her animals. But more than that, more than anything else in the world, Marilee wanted to be rich enough so that the snobby girls at school would stop making fun of her and she could buy any dress she wanted for winter formal.

Then, the guy she wanted would definitely ask her to be his date.

But she never, ever dreamed that it would happen.

About the Authors

CHERIE BENNETT and JEFF GOTTESFELD have co-written many well-loved series for teens, including *Teen Angels, Sunset Island, Wild Hearts,* and now *Mirror Image.* Cherie also writes hardcover fiction, including the award-winning *Life in the Fat Lane* and *Zink.* She is also one of America's finest young playwrights *(Anne Frank & Me; Searching for David's Heart),* a two-time New Visions/New Voices play-writing winner at the Kennedy Center. Her Copley News Service teen advice column, *Hey, Cherie!,* is syndicated nationally. Cherie and Jeff celebrate their tenth anniversary next year; they live in Los Angeles and Nashville. Contact them at P.O. Box 150326, Nashville, TN 37215; or authorchik@aol.com.